Fearfully ~~Frightening~~

What is that noise in the chimney? Why did the car leave no tyre tracks on the muddy road? What is causing Mr Cook's mysterious illness? Ten spine-chilling stories in which young people confront phantoms, spirits, ghosts or aliens from other worlds. Chosen especially for readers of nine and upwards and guaranteed to make your hair stand on end.

This is Barbara Ireson's fourth collection of ghost stories for Beaver Books. The others are: *Ghostly and Ghastly, Creepy Creatures*, and *Ghostly Laughter*.

FEARFULLY FRIGHTENING

Chosen by Barbara Ireson

Beaver Books

A Beaver Original
Published by Arrow Publications
17–21 Conway Street, London W1P 6JD
A division of the Hutchinson Publishing Group
London Melbourne Sydney Auckland Johannesburg
and agencies throughout the world

First published in 1984
© Copyright this collection Barbara Ireson 1984
© Copyright illustrations Beaver Books 1984

Set in Baskerville
Printed and bound in Great Britain by
Anchor Brendon Limited, Tiptree, Essex

ISBN 0 09 933770 3

Contents

The Ghost of Rainbow Hill

Margaret Biggs

'We're late,' Mum said, glancing at her watch anxiously. She accelerated jumpily. 'I wish I could have got away earlier. Still, we should be able to make good time now we're into the country.'

I sat beside her, in charge of the map, feeling slightly sick as I always did when she drove me in the Mini. School had broken up that day for half-term, and Mum was driving me down to stay with Gran for the week. Mum worked full-time, and in the holidays I found our small flat cramped and, after a while, boring. I had read every book we possessed, and got sick of watching TV very soon. It was better staying with Gran: she always welcomed me with flatteringly open arms, and let me go my own way. She and I got on well, being alike in our dislike of being bossed. Mum and I tended to argue and fight. Mum was OK, but she still treated me as a child, and nobody at nearly thirteen likes that. But I made allowances for her, because I knew how lonely she was since Dad died. She had to let off steam sometimes.

I looked at my watch. Nearly half-past six. I wondered again what Gran's new place would be like. She'd recently moved into part of an old Georgian house, called Rainbow Hall, deep in the hills. The name intrigued me, and Gran's letter telling me all about it had been glowing and, for her, unusually enthusiastic: 'I wish I'd moved here out of London years ago, Jacky, just as people kept telling me to. You'll love this huge wild garden, and I know you'll enjoy exploring the house. It used to belong to some people called Merryfield, before it was turned into flats, and they were horse-mad, which should interest you. The stables are huge, we keep logs and things in them, and you can wander wherever you like. There's a rather fascinating story about a boy who used to live here and his mare, called Tara, which I'll tell you about. . . .' It sounded promising. I adored horses, though I've never had the chance to ride, and I loved old gardens.

'Is it left here, Jacky?' Mum asked.

She switched on the headlights. The beams blazed down the silent road. It was lonely here, miles from anywhere, and Mum was always a bit nervous when she was out of town and in unknown territory.

'Yes, left, and then down a steep hill – how funny, it's called Rainbow Hill,' I said, peering at the large-scale map. 'Then we're nearly there.'

'Thank heaven,' Mum muttered. I knew she had a headache. 'I hate these country roads with no lights, all bends and twists.' She turned the corner. 'This must be the top of the hill. Heavens, it's certainly steep – you're right there.'

A drizzle of rain began spattering the windscreen, and Mum hastily clicked on the wipers. It had gone dark suddenly. They drummed against the window, and Mum leaned forward screwing up her eyes to get a better view. Again she accelerated, and I knew she was tired and wanted to get there, but wished she wasn't in such a hurry. But she nearly always was....

Rainbow Hill was steep as the swing downwards on the Big Dipper. Our headlights cut a swathe through the rain and dark, and I was thankful there was no other traffic. It was as if we were the only people left on earth. I half-closed my eyes and leaned back, looking at the pale moon swimming up between the drifting clouds. I took deep breaths, trying to get rid of my sick feeling. Then suddenly Mum shouted: 'Oh my God, look!' and jammed on the brakes. The car juddered and slid on the slippery road, wheels screeching, and as I jerked forward, my eyes wide open again, I saw another car racing straight across in front of us. It was an old-fashioned open-topped green two-seater, and at the wheel sat a boy gripping it, his red hair blown hectically in the wind, white-faced, his eyes staring straight ahead with enormous intensity.

'We're going to hit him!' Mum shouted, sounding the horn desperately.

The boy never glanced in our direction, never seemed aware of us, though how could he not be? He drove straight across our path a bare few yards ahead, and was gone. We slithered to a halt sideways. Mum's hands were shaking. 'That crazy boy, he came straight out of that side lane – we could all have been killed!' she cried, wildly indignant, and flung open the door. We jumped out, both scared and bewildered. Mum gripped my arm, and I gazed in the direction the two-seater had gone. It was a T-junction, with a lane joining Rainbow Hill near the bottom. But now Mum had switched off our engine everything was uncannily silent, save for the drone of traffic far away on the main road, and a cow mooing mournfully in a field nearby. There was no sign of the boy's car, not even his red back light, and no noise of his engine.

'He must have been going incredibly fast,' I said, gazing down the dark empty lane.

'He ought to be prosecuted, shooting out like that,' Mum was saying. 'Are you all right, Jacky? What's the matter?'

I had bent down to look at the wet road. 'That's funny. Look, Mum, there aren't any tyre marks going across at all. Only ours, coming downhill.'

'That's impossible,' Mum said flatly. But she had to agree. If we had not both seen the car, we would have thought we had been dreaming. After a minute or two, not knowing what else to do we got back into our car and drove on, slowly now, mulling it over, puzzled, mystified, Mum taking extra care at every bend and junction.

'The lane must have been dry,' Mum said, trying to convince herself.

'You could see it was wet,' I answered.

We were silent until we reached the drive leading to Rainbow Hall, a mile or two further on. It was pitch-dark now and the drive snaked between trees which leaned low across, branches scraping the car roof as we drove beneath. There was an eerie feel about it, I thought, but decided not to say so. Mum was quite worked up enough.

'Your gran's certainly picked an out-of-the-way spot to live – rather her than me,' Mum commented. Then she said: 'Oh good, here's the house!' as a big grey house swam into view in our headlights, with imposing white pillars shining in the night.

'And there's Gran!' I said, as Gran appeared between the pillars, an umbrella waving wildly at us. I felt better as soon as I saw her face.

In a couple of minutes we were inside Rainbow Hall, and the wet cold night was shut out. Gran fussed round us, making coffee, cutting slices of home-made chocolate cake, asking all sorts of questions. Her flat was warm and snug, with all her familiar ornaments and family pictures, and I was pleased to see Mum relaxing visibly, and obviously feeling soothed. Gran had this effect – she never got excited herself. Soon they were chatting, catching up on family news. I wandered round, coffee mug in hand, looking at things, calming down again. Suddenly I pulled up. There on Gran's mantelpiece was a framed photo, rather faded. I stared unbelievingly at it.

'Gran – who's this?'

Gran looked round, surprised at my urgency. 'Why, that's the boy I was going to tell you about, Jacky. His name's Rafe Merryfield, and that's his mare Tara beside him. He lived in this house years ago.'

'But that's the boy who was driving the car we just nearly crashed into!' I carried the photo across to Mum. 'Look, it *is*, isn't it?'

She took a reluctant look and admitted cautiously: 'It might be. But it couldn't have been. That looks like a very old photograph.'

'It is. He was killed in a road accident near Rainbow Hill, at least fifty years ago,' Gran said quietly. She looked at our stunned faces. 'Tell me what happened, and then I'll tell you what I know about him.'

We told her briefly, Mum saying as little as

possible, and after a moment Gran sighed. 'So you've seen him too!' Her face looked compassionate and sombre. 'Other people round here have, as well. His sister still lives here, in one of the flats, and she's a friend of mine. It was she who lent me the photo, because I wanted to show it to Jacky, and tell her all about it. It's so sad, and I know how Jacky loves a sad story, especially with a horse in it.'

Mum looked uneasy, but I commanded: 'Tell me, Gran,' plumping down beside her on the settee. 'Go on, what happened?'

'Is this a good idea?' Mum said dubiously.

'I'll just tell you, and then we'll talk about something else,' Gran said, smiling at my eager face. 'Jacky will get it out of me!'

Rafe Merryfield's family had loved horses, Gran said. They had lived at the Hall for two generations, and bred them. Out of them all Tara had been Rafe's favourite, his own mare, a beautiful shy glossy chestnut. She had been born here, on the estate, and as soon as she was old enough Rafe trained her and rode her everywhere. He was very possessive about her. 'His sister told me all this.' Then, one autumn day, he had been out riding her, and jumping a fence in the twilight on his way home, quite near the house, Tara had made a mistake and they had fallen heavily and awkwardly. Rafe was knocked out, and when he came round he found Tara lying still beside him, unconscious. He felt her all over, but it was getting too dark to see properly. He could only tell she was breathing. He was terrified she might have broken her back. He left her and, bruised as he was, dashed across the fields and into the stable-yard. He revved up his father's sports car, which his father had just parked ten minutes before, and drove off like a mad thing for the vet, who lived in the village on the other side of Rainbow Hill. They had no telephone.

Rafe's sister was in the stables and she came running out when she heard Rafe. He looked ghastly, she said, with mud on his face. He shouted to her to get a blanket and find Tara and keep her warm, but not to try to move her whatever happened. 'I've got to get help straight away – she's *got* to be all right!' he yelled. Then he drove off at top speed, like a maniac, she said, shooting up the drive like a rocket. She was terrified he'd hit someone, but she did what he told her and found Tara across the fields and wrapped her in a blanket and waited beside her. Rafe had only driven the car once or twice before. In those days there was no driving test. Still, the vet only lived two miles away, so she prayed Rafe would get to him in time safely.

Gran paused. 'Oh, go on,' I urged.

She looked at the ancient photograph, and I looked as well. Rafe's arm was round Tara's sturdy neck, and his cheek was pressed against her. He looked radiantly proud and happy. 'You can guess, love. He overturned the car just beyond Rainbow Hill, and was flung out and killed instantly.'

'Oh, that's tragic,' Mum said, despite herself.

'But Tara? What about her?' I cut in eagerly.

'She was all right. She'd been stunned, nothing more, the vet said, when he examined her later. That was after Rafe had been killed.'

'So the crash was all for nothing. How awful,' I said, feeling acutely the waste of it all. It really *was* a sad story, and I felt deeply for Rafe. My heart ached, guessing a little of how he must have felt.

'The family never got over it. They sold up and left the district. But Rafe's sister still lives here, as I told you. She came back here after years abroad. She often talks about the old days, as she calls them. She idolised Rafe. If only he'd known Tara wasn't dying! she often says.'

'I'm positive that was a real car we saw, not a ghost, as you're implying,' Mum cut in, in a determined tone. 'It must have been a coincidence. Another boy, in a similar car.'

'Perhaps so, dear,' Gran said in her non-committal way. 'It was about half-past six he was killed,' she added, and I shivered, remembering looking at my watch just before we saw the car.

'I insist we talk about something else,' Mum said, sticking her chin out. 'Jacky will be having one of her nightmares!'

'I haven't had one for years,' I said indignantly.

'Never mind – you forget all about this – and Mother, please don't encourage her,' Mum said.

'Of course not, dear,' Gran said peaceably. 'Don't worry – have some more coffee.' And the talk branched away. But though I listened I kept on thinking about Rafe.

Mum set off again for home after a quick meal, for she had to work next day. She gave me a swift warm hug and said: 'Have a good time, Jacky. I'll be down next weekend to pick you up. Get plenty of fresh air – you look peaky.'

'Don't worry about me, I'm fine,' I said hastily. 'Take care going home.'

She nodded. 'I'm not going via Rainbow Hill, I can tell you!' And she hurried off, before I could tell her how illogical she was. For if she didn't believe in ghosts, why avoid the hill?

I approved of the bedroom Gran gave me. It was a big room next to hers and looked out across towards the stables, she said, and the garden. When she had said goodnight and left me I padded around, looking at everything, then opened the sash window and leaned out. It had stopped raining and the night air smelt fresh and cool. Trees shook their branches near the window, and there was an immense quiet all round. 'I do like it here,' I thought.

Yet when I got into bed I couldn't sleep for ages. There was a heavy sad feeling all round me, and I couldn't get Rafe out of my head, though I tried. He felt close somehow. If I only knew exactly where he was, I felt I could have put out my hand and touched him. I shivered at the thought, and huddled low down under the blankets, pulling them tightly round me. When at last I fell asleep I dreamt of Rafe. I saw him vividly, cantering across a meadow, riding Tara. It was a silent scene, like watching an old film. He was smiling, obviously happy, his red hair shining in the sun. He leaned forward to pat Tara's shiny neck, holding the reins easily. The mare was going steadily, obviously enjoying herself, the pair of them moving as one. She really was a beauty. I could feel the bond between them as I watched in my dream. I saw Rafe arriving at Rainbow Hall, sliding off Tara's back, feeding her a lump of sugar before unsaddling her. I saw the mare rest her head on his shoulder, nuzzling him as he unbuckled the saddle-girths. Then my dream dissolved and faded.

When I woke the birds were calling sleepily. It was early, and the light was still grey at the window. I lay still, and the conviction came into my head: 'This was Rafe's room.' I was sure of it. Rafe had slept here years ago, and his spirit still lingered, reluctant to leave. As I lay there, my eyes half shut, again Rafe seemed very near. I wished I could get through to him and tell him: 'It's all right, Rafe, Tara didn't die. You didn't let her down, crashing the car.' I tried to send the message silently, inside my head, to Rafe, repeating it over and over again. Then I dozed off.

'Gran,' I said at breakfast, 'I do like Rainbow Hall. Can I explore round the garden this morning?'

'You go where you like, love. Nobody will stop you.' Gran looked smilingly at me, and I was relieved she seldom asked questions, like Mum, who sometimes worried and probed unnecessarily.

'That car Mum and I saw last night,' I said, fiddling with a knife, 'Do you know if many other people have seen it?'

Gran pursed her lips. 'It's an open sports car, green, isn't it? Yes, quite a few, so they say. Not many people are alive now who remember the Merryfields, and some have moved away, but I've spoken to several who knew them. Rafe seemed everyone's favourite. A grand lad he must have been – friendly, cheerful, always whistling, stopping to chat to whomever he met. Everyone liked him. That's why the accident was such a tragedy.'

I hesitated, but I had to ask. 'Do *you* believe in ghosts, Gran?'

'I don't disbelieve in them, love. We don't know all the answers, though we sometimes think we do.'

I thought the same. The car with Rafe inside didn't frighten me at all: it only made me feel sad, made me yearn to help him. Rafe can't rest, because he feels he let Tara die, I thought. The story's still unfinished. He's still trying to get help for her somehow, after all these years, and still failing.

I went into the stables after helping Gran wash up. Nobody was about, and my footsteps echoed on the stone flags. Dusty bits of tack hung on the walls.

Huge spiders' webs stirred in the breeze as I opened the door. Empty, whitewashed, the stables still smelt of horses. I wondered where Rafe had groomed Tara, which had been her stall. In our flat there was not a spare inch: yet here in the stables there was room and to spare. How I wished I had lived at Rainbow Hall in the old carefree days, before things went wrong! Perhaps Rafe might have let me sit on Tara: perhaps I might even have learned to ride. That was an old dream, for we couldn't afford riding lessons, as I knew perfectly well. I had to make do with reading about ponies, and sometimes dreaming about them. Perhaps it was because of that that I couldn't get Rafe and Tara out of my head. They seemed to take possession of me.

There was an old bike leaning against one wall, and as I looked at it, wondering vaguely whose it was, a shadow fell across me. I looked up startled to see an elderly woman, older even than Gran, watching me. She had a thin weather-beaten face, intent eyes, and grey hair with glints of red in it.

'Hello,' she said. 'You must be Jacky. Your grandmother's told me about you. Are you having a look round? I'm Miss Merryfield. I remember when these stables were full of horses.' She looked round as if she could see invisible horses in the empty stalls.

Of course, she must be Rafe's sister. How stupid, I'd expected her to be young. . . . It made me realise how long ago the accident had happened, long before my mother had been born.

'What happened to Tara?' I blurted.

Luckily she wasn't offended, and she didn't seem surprised at the question. 'Oh, I kept her till she died. She lived to a ripe old age. She was quite happy, but I know she was always hoping Rafe would come back. She would sometimes stop dead and look over her shoulder and wait, then go on again. She never forgot him.'

I nodded. I was sure that was true. Miss Merryfield and I stood looking at each other as if we were old friends, which was strange, because usually I hate talking to strangers.

'That's my bike,' she said in her abrupt way. 'It's a bit of a wreck, but you're welcome to borrow it while you're here. It's not as much fun as a horse, but at least it will get you about.'

'Oh, thank you,' I said. 'That would be great.'

She nodded, gave me a brief searching look, then smiled and went off again. She's almost like a ghost herself, I thought. I like her, she's different, she doesn't say ordinary boring things like most grownups.

I found Rainbow Hall a lovely place to mooch about in. Nobody bothered me. I seldom saw the people in the other flats, for they were all elderly and stayed in most of the time. It seemed as if the whole place had been waiting for me. The sun-warmed brick wall round the old kitchen garden, the deserted greenhouses with their creaking, swinging doors, the big fish-pond choked with weed, a few jewel-bright fish gliding deep down: everything seemed to be there just for me. Inside the house I felt I knew my way. My feet clattered on the wooden stairs as if they knew where to go, and my hand slid comfortably along the worn wooden rail. It was a Sleeping Beauty place, that had suddenly stopped short in its tracks, and was waiting – for what? All the time Rafe seemed near. Sometimes I was sure I would meet him when I turned a corner. Once or twice I could have sworn I heard him whistling. His presence was strongest in my bedroom. Sometimes I lay reading on the bed while Gran was resting, and after a few minutes I knew he was there. The sad feeling would swamp me, and I would give up my book and lie with my eyes shut, just thinking. And gradually, imperceptibly, my thoughts crystallised into a plan.

I only had this one week. Mum would be coming for me on Saturday. I couldn't go away without at least trying. It might be no good, but I had to try. I had the absurd feeling that I was the person the house, and Rafe, had been waiting for all these years.

I dusted down Miss Merryfield's old bike, pumped up the tyres, and after tea on Friday, my last free day, told Gran I was going for just a short ride.

'All right, love,' Gran said equably, pouring out another cup of tea. 'Remember it's dark by seven, won't you? And don't get lost.'

'I'll be all right,' I promised.

I set off down the drive. It was already growing gloomy under the trees, and I wished the bike had lights. A branch brushed my face and made me jump. It was like a hand grabbing at me.

It was simple to find the way back to Rainbow Hill. I only had to follow the road from the gate for a mile or so. Then I took a track across the fields, signposted 'Rainbow Hill, ½ mile', which was a short cut to the top of the hill, I knew. Which way would Rafe have driven on that desperate night? Not this path, it wasn't wide enough for a car. He would have driven further down the road, then taken the lane that cut sharply at right angles across the bottom of the hill, accelerating towards the village where the vet lived!

I had to get the time just right – to be at the top of

the hill a minute or two before half-past six. That was vital.

Rainbow Hill was silent, as before, when I reached it. There was a high thorn hedge on either side, blotting out the fields. The sky was beginning to darken, and a farm dog was barking away across the fields, but I heard no other sound. There was no wind tonight: the trees stood utterly still, like sentinels watching me. My mouth was dry, I felt scared and gulped. Probably nothing at all would happen. It was just a chance, nothing to be scared of, I told myself scathingly. Gripping the handlebars tightly I checked it was coming up to half-past six, and began to cycle downhill. I didn't freewheel, but pedalled fast, to get up a good speed. My heart was thudding behind my ribs.

Now! I muttered over and over under my breath. Now, Rafe! Now! *Now*!

As I had half-hoped, half-feared, it happened. The air blew sharply cold against my face, my hair streamed out behind me, and as I neared the bottom of the hill, I saw the green car come shooting out just in front of me. It made no sound – it moved silently but at what seemed to me a superhuman speed. I was terrified but exulted. I was almost on top of it, almost within touching distance. I could see Rafe's chalk-white face clearly, in detail, far nearer than before. I saw his white knuckles as he gripped the wheel, his unwavering desperate stare, even the mud on his cheek from his fall. This was it, my chance. I squeezed the brakes hard and shouted at the top of my voice: 'Rafe, Rafe, it's all right! Tara's all right, she's perfectly all right! You didn't let her die! You needn't worry any more!'

My voice came out in a shriek. Was it my over-excited imagination, or did Rafe turn his head towards me? I had only a second to wonder. Then the bike skidded as I braked, turned sideways and crashed heavily into the hedge. I was thrown hard into the midst of spiky twigs and branches, and passed out.

I came to almost at once, bruised and shaking. My legs felt wobbly as blancmange. I was utterly exhausted, for some reason. I pulled the bike out of the hedge with some difficulty, and brushed myself down. Then I looked along the lane. But I was alone, with gathering darkness my only companion. I felt limp, and I had no idea if I had done any good. Probably not. Probably it had all been a waste of time. I was lucky I hadn't hurt myself for nothing, and poor Mum would have been so upset if she'd known. Too shaken to get on again, I wheeled the bike slowly back across the fields. It clanked. I wanted to get indoors, to be fussed over by Gran, to shut out the unknown and forget about Rafe. It was suddenly all too much for me, this strange link-up with the past.

I pushed wearily up the drive, pitch-dark now. My legs were scratched from the hedge, despite my jeans, which were torn at one knee, and a scratch on my forehead was bleeding. I rubbed at it as I went along. I was vastly relieved when the mass of the house loomed up before me. I tramped round to the stables, dumped the bike, and then went straight up to my bedroom. I had to wash and tidy myself up before seeing Gran – I didn't want her getting worried, and I didn't feel up to long explanations.

I knew as soon as I came into the bedroom. It felt clear, relieved, shiningly happy. That blanket of sadness had blown away. And it felt utterly empty at last. I slumped down on the bed and let the feeling of content wash over me. Rafe knew: he had heard me, and he was at peace at last. It was worth all my aches and pains.

Gran told me, in a letter months later, that nobody had ever seen Rafe's car again.

The Lost Gold Mine

Hazel F. Looker

South Wales is famous for its steam-coal and anthracite; old lead mines are scattered among the hills of mid-Wales, and there is gold, too. True, Wales has never known a gold rush, as there is far too little gold for that, but the fever can take hold of anyone, and once it gets into the blood it drives a man on until he finds gold or dies in the attempt.

There was only one small hotel in Tresaint (pronounced Sant); it had about eight bedrooms, and kept a very good table. There was also pony trekking in the village, and some of the trekkers stayed at the hotel, while others either camped out or found accommodation in the neighbouring farms and cottages.

Sue Milbrook and her two friends, Richard Price and Tim Westgate, had booked early, so they had rooms at the hotel, and, having travelled down in Sue's car, were all set to enjoy their last holiday together. They had just completed their college courses, and each would soon be embarking on his or her own career.

Sue was a good rider and had her own pony back home, but the two boys had yet to discover the joys of horsemanship. Sue had worked up their enthusiasm, telling them of the views from the hills which no motorist ever saw, of the peace that comes when one is seated on a sure-footed pony following some moorland track, and the fun with fellow trekkers.

'You need proper riding breeches,' she said. 'That's important, otherwise you'll get sore between the knees if you are riding properly. Good boots, too, because you often have to "squelch" through bogs. Some people wear riding hats, but I'm not taking mine, it gives me a headache. I always wear gloves though – stops my hands from getting sore and dirty.'

Over the washbasin in each bedroom hung a card giving information of meal times and places of interest in the locality. Tresaint, it informed them, meant Three Saints, so called because three Celtic Saints had rested here on their way to found a priory. The stone on which they sat could still be seen, hollowed out where each Saint had rested. There was also a gold mine worked in Roman times which was worth a visit.

Tim, who had taken Economic Geography as one of his special subjects at college, was interested in rocks. In fact, he had often thought of becoming a geologist and getting a job prospecting for some big company. His aim was to get rich quick if he could, and, while not being exactly mean, he hated parting with money; at the end of term he was always the one left with something in the bank. This old gold mine interested him, and he made a mental note to visit it at the first opportunity.

While waiting for the others to join him in the bar

before dinner that evening he asked the landlord how far it was to the gold mine.

'Oh, not far,' the landlord replied. 'You go down to the bridge, turn left at the next fork opposite the chapel, then go on up the lane till you come to a big farm, and right opposite there you'll see the Saints' stone — it's on the grass verge. You can't miss it.'

'I'm not interested in the stone,' Tim retorted. 'Where's the gold mine?'

'If you'll give me a chance, I'll tell you,' the land-lord frowned. 'Climb up a steep bank that's just behind the stone, and over the top you'll see the old workings.'

'Thank you,' said Tim, and finished his beer just as his friends appeared.

'Let's go in to dinner right away,' he urged, 'then we'll have time for a stroll before it gets too dark.'

As soon as dinner was over he led the way in the direction indicated by the landlord, but after some twenty minutes Sue said: 'Let's go back now, I'm tired after all that driving.'

'It isn't far now,' Tim insisted.

'What isn't far?' Richard asked.

'The gold mine, I want to have a look at it.'

'Oh, all right,' Sue agreed with some reluctance, 'but you haven't been driving all day as I have.'

They turned a bend in the lane, and after descending an incline came to what appeared to be a village green; to the left of this were cultivated fields, and on the right they found the stone. It was hollowed out into three seats.

Tim gave the stone a kick. 'Three Saints indeed,' he said scornfully, 'I've seen stones like this in Cornwall. The old tin miners used them for washing the stuff they brought out of the mine, and in time water wore hollows in the stone, like these, and then they turned it over and used the other side.'

He took a run up the high bank, and found himself looking down into a kind of amphitheatre. The bank of debris formed a half-circle on the mountainside, and at the bottom Tim saw the entrance to the mine. It was a tunnel hewn out of the solid rock, and appeared to be about two feet deep in water.

'It must have taken them ages to cut into that rock with their primitive tools,' said Sue.

'They were great engineers, the Romans,' Richard remarked, 'I mean, think of all those marvellous aqueducts they built.'

Tim did not comment. His one desire was to get down into that tunnel and examine the rock, but he knew it was no use asking the others to wait any longer, so he decided to come again on his own and have a really good look round.

Next morning they found the paddock where the ponies were being saddled bustling with trekkers clad in every conceivable type of riding kit, ranging from the immaculate to jeans-and-Wellington-boots. Sue helped her friends to saddle and bridle their ponies, and showed them how to tighten the girth because, as she explained: 'Ponies blow out their bellies when you put the saddle on, and if you don't tighten up it might slip round and you'll perhaps end up under the horse's belly.'

At last they were ready, and set off through the village looking rather like Chaucer's pilgrims on their way to Canterbury. Sue laughed as she watched some novices cling to their saddle with one hand, while others held the reins high and tight, making the poor ponies' necks arch.

'Never have so many suffered so much at the hands of those who know so little,' she misquoted.

However, confidence grew as they journeyed on, for Twm Trek, as the guide was called, took it easy on this first day. Soon they were up on the mountain tracks, relaxed and able to chat with one another as the sure-footed animals picked their way over the rough stones or boggy places. Tim caught up with the guide and offered him a cigarette.

'It's not too bad up here today,' said Twm as he lit up. 'We've had a lot of rain lately, and after a wet spring things can be a bit dicey sometimes. I've seen trekkers come off in a bog and come out covered in black mud. They've had to let it dry and then peel it off in chunks.' He chuckled. 'These little ponies are good, though, they can pick their own way if you let them. Horses would be no good up here, sir.'

Tim, after a while, remarked casually: 'The old gold mine – am I to understand it is completely worked out?'

'Yes, indeed,' Twm nodded. 'The seam was worked out long ago, but they do say it grew richer and richer, then suddenly stopped. No more gold, just plain old rock.'

It was Tim's turn to nod. 'The rock must have split and one part slipped down. But surely with all the modern instruments we have nowadays it should be possible to find the seam again?'

'Oh, lots of people have tried from time to time,' Twm said, 'but none of them had any luck. Though if the old tale be true there is a way of finding it.'

'How?' asked Tim breathlessly.

The guide did not answer for some little while, then he began to speak in a quiet tone as though he were revealing some secret; like a man reluctantly uncovering a family skeleton to the morbid gaze of a stranger. 'Now look you, this yarn has been passed down from father to son, and maybe it's all eyewash, although there are those today who swear it's all true. But it is said that a long time ago the rich seam was found, and work started on it, then something happened. A terrible disaster like, all the miners died, nobody knows how, but no living thing came back, neither men nor ponies – they used ponies like these to cart the stuff away, see.'

'How dreadful.' Tim felt he could do no more than make some such remark.

'Yes,' the guide nodded, 'if it was true, it must have been dreadful. But this is the story you wanted to hear. They, the old ones you understand, say that on some nights if you go up the lane by the chapel you'll see the ponies making their way to the new seam. If a man wants gold bad enough, all he has to do is to follow them.'

'And has anyone ever followed them?' Tim inquired after a while.

'Yes,' Twm said shortly, then added, 'or so it is said.'

'And . . .?'

The guide turned his head and looked the young man full in the face.

'They never came back.'

Tim, despite his modern, matter-of-fact outlook, felt a shiver run down his spine, then he laughed.

'Sure you don't believe any of this?'

Twm nudged his horse forward.

'Maybe I don't,' he said, and terminated the conversation by riding a little way ahead, leaving a very thoughtful young man behind him.

Next morning Tim announced he was not joining the trek.

'I'm disgusted with you,' said Sue, 'giving up so soon. The stiffness will wear off once you get back into the saddle.'

'It's not that,' Tim said, 'I promise I'll come tomorrow, but there's something I must do today.'

'Please yourself,' Sue walked away, her head held high, for she liked people to do what she wanted, and the boys, being of an easy going nature, usually followed her lead. Tim grimaced, then set off in the direction of the old gold mine. He climbed the bank, then trudged down the incline to the tunnel cut into the mountainside; the water was fully two feet deep, clear as a washed window pane, but, as he found out once he had removed his shoes and socks and waded in, extremely cold. He reached up and tried to pull a sample of rock from the low roof, but he could find no loose fragments. Spotting a jagged stone lying on a narrow ledge, he used this as a hammer, and finally managed to collect a few good specimens. They were brownish-yellow in colour, but there was no suggestion they might contain gold ore. He followed the course of the tunnel some twenty yards into the mountainside, using the torch he had thoughtfully brought with him, but here he was brought to a halt by a fall of rock which completely blocked the passage.

He retraced his footsteps and, once back in the open air, removed his drenched trousers and laid them out in the sun to dry, then sat down and tried to reason out just where the new seam, always supposing it existed, could have been located. It could possibly have been somewhere beyond that fall of rock; that being the case, without elaborate machinery he had no hope of reaching it. This could well have been the disaster that had overcome the long-dead miners, a sudden cave-in, burying men and ponies. But if that had happened, surely some effort would have been made to get them out, or recover their remains. No, he was certain the new workings were farther afield, but the question was, where? On one side there was the mountain, over to the east was a vast swamp, to the north, open moorland. That must be the answer, out there in that desolate waste; the home of the moorhen, where the occasional tree bowed its head to the prevailing wind as though begging alms from the sun, and the rough heather-clad earth glowered up at the benign sky. Tim Westgate rose quickly, pulled on his still damp trousers, discarded his usually much-valued commonsense, and went out on to the moor. The gold fever was in his bloodstream.

He wandered a long way that day, climbing hills, peering into grass-choked hollows, never really believing he would find that which he sought, but unable to give up the search which his reasoning powers vainly tried to tell him was a complete waste of time. He lunched at a moorland inn, a small dismal place ruled over by a dour landlord who seemed to resent this stranger demanding refreshment, then went forth again on his seemingly endless quest.

Night was sending its dark shadow over the moor before he returned to the realms of sanity; he looked over to the western horizon and saw the flaming rim of the sun, felt the icy fingers of the night wind and tasted fear. To be lost on the moor at night was no joke, and he began to make his way towards the now distant mountain, praying that he might reach the village before complete darkness fell. In fact his fears were groundless, a full moon was painting the old chapel with a silver glow when he entered the lane, footsore, tired to the state of exhaustion, but thankful his journey was almost over.

'I was mad,' he told himself, 'mad. As though one could hope to find gold in twentieth-century Wales.'

He passed the chapel and had reached the end of the lane when he heard the sound. A soft padding, then a clip-clop, followed by the rattle of harness. Tim began to shiver; he felt the short hairs on the back of his neck begin to rise as he remembered the story told to him by Twm Trek.

The ponies came out from nowhere. First the head, then the shoulders, finally a complete pony emerged from a position roughly in the centre of the lane; it was as though it had come through an invisible curtain. Tim flattened himself against the wall as another pony followed the first, then another; presently a long file were trudging up the lane, some carrying picks and trenching tools strapped to their backs, others bearing empty sacks or long, sharp-pointed stakes. Tim was shivering with terror, but somewhere, from the back of his fear-crazed brain, a thought sprang into being and would not be ignored. If he were to follow this phantom file, would they not lead him to the new seam? A vision of himself at the head of a gold-mining company; wealth, power, position – fear began to recede before a rising lust for gold.

The last pony passed him, and almost against his will Tim left the security of the wall and began to follow the ghostly line. The clink of harness, the soft pad of hoofs, an occasional snort, Tim could scarcely belief this was not a file of living animals wending their way towards the open moor. Then, with another blast of icy fear, he realised they cast no shadow; the full moon highlighted the brown or black rumps, gilded the metal trappings on harness or trenching tools, but there were no silhouettes, no evidence of solid bodies intruding between moonlight and earth.

They skirted the lower slopes of the mountain, passed the old mine entrance, then proceeded on down an incline towards a cluster of wind-bowed trees.

'Downhill, of course.' Excitement bubbled in Tim's fevered brain. 'They did not try to follow the seam deeper into the mountain, they went back to its source. The beginning.'

The first pony disappeared into the deep shadow that lurked beneath the trees; the others followed, seemingly guided by invisible hands. When Tim at last entered the eerie gloom he found his progress was hampered by dense undergrowth. It seemed there was an active force trying to hold him back; brambles clung to his legs, encircled his waist, and he swore as he wrenched himself free, only to bark his shins on a fallen branch, walk into a low bush, whose whippy branches seemed determined to beat him back. All the while he could hear the ponies trudging sedately ahead. Once, when a gap in the overhead treetops permitted the moonlight a sparse entrance, he had a glimpse of the last animal moving effortlessly through a thick bush.

When he emerged from that nightmare wood, his face and hands were covered with weals and scratches, but he gave a joyful cry when he saw the line of ponies crossing what appeared to be a smooth, grass-carpeted expanse of open country. They were now some forty yards away, and Tim broke into a run, determined to catch them up, certain that by now he must be within reach of his Mecca – the new workings.

The earth reached up and clutched his feet; there was an awful sucking sound, an obscene squelching, and he began to sink down into that treacherous green carpet. He struggled, an action that only made his predicament worse, for now the mire was up to his thighs, and the sucking, squelching sounds were like evil chuckles as the bog drew him deeper into its embrace. Even now he could not entirely forget the receding ponies. They too were going down into the bog, but they were walking as though down an incline, and Tim laughed aloud, a mad shriek as the last pony disappeared from view.

'So that's where it is. Under thirty or forty feet of bloody, life-sucking bog.'

He was down to his waist when he began to scream, long drawn out shrieks that ran out across the moor, and the moon gazed down at him with her cold, silver-hued face, like a beautiful woman disdainfully ignoring the pleading of a discarded lover. The mire had reached his armpits before he again heard the sound of approaching ponies' hoofs, and he screamed his terror-inspired rage.

'You've got me, there's no need to come back.'

'Tim!'

The voice came out of yesterday; from the far-off world of sanity, where young men did not follow ghostly ponies and flounder in Welsh bogs. He turned his head and saw Sue and Richard standing a few yards away; the boy's face was strained and white, but Sue wore an expression of grim determination. She snapped:

'Richard, quick, fetch a long branch!'

'But . . .' Richard could not tear his terror-stricken gaze from Tim's three-quarter submerged form.

Sue shouted again: 'Don't stand there, fetch a long branch!'

After Richard had departed, she spoke soothingly to Tim.

'Don't move. Keep absolutely still. It's your only chance.'

It was fifteen minutes before they pulled him out, for the bog was reluctant to part with a victim, and when he finally lay on firm ground, Tim gasped out his thanks.

'I knew something had gone wrong when you didn't return at sunset,' Sue said. 'Suddenly I remembered the bog, though why on earth you should want to come down here is beyond me. Didn't you see the signs?'

'I was following the ponies.'

'What ponies?' Sue demanded.

'Never mind.' He sighed and then looked out across the deceptively smooth green surface. 'The disaster must have been water. Perhaps they uncovered a giant underground spring or something.'

'Let's get you back to the hotel.' Sue looked more than a little worried. 'You're probably running a fever.'

Tim shook his head.

'Not now,' he said, 'not now.'

The Ghost of Gartenschmuck

Colin Thiele

The ghost of *Gartenschmuck* was more than a legend. It was a real thing. For thirty years it had been appearing near the main road from Kapunda to Bethel, not far from the grim old house in the Valley.

Some people said there were actually two ghosts – one a tender, womanly spirit like a column of white light, and the other a monstrous ghoul that had almost killed poor Ahmed Singh, the hawker, when he had accidentally camped in *Gartenschmuck* one night long ago before he'd heard that it was haunted. The tender one was the ghost of Maria Rollenberg, a lovely bride who had been murdered on her wedding night thirty years before by her husband, Kreutzer, who himself had then come to a bad end. *Gartenschmuck* was the house they were going to live in after the wedding. It remained empty ever afterwards – a huge sombre place with endless sheds and barns and sties surrounding it like an old fortress or medieval keep. Nobody ever went near it except the Richter boys, who owned the farm now. But even they made sure they were gone before the sun set.

Benny Geister lived with his Uncle Gus a few kilometres away near the foothills, and his best friend, Ossie Schmidt, came from the farm next door. Benny was twelve and Ossie was thirteen, but nobody knew how old Uncle Gus was. They had all seen the ghost of Maria Rollenberg; in fact Uncle Gus had seen it so often that he had lost count. Twice his horse had bolted when the ghost had confronted them on their way home from the Morning Star Hotel in the midnight moonlight, and once he had actually run over it in his old Ford. But none of them had ever seen the ghost of Kreutzer. Ossie said this was because it never came out into the open, but kept skulking about in the shadows of *Gartenschmuck*.

'He's a nasty piece of work, Kreutzer is,' Ossie said with authority one day. 'Very nasty and silent.'

'How do you know?' Benny asked.

'Because he got Ahmed Singh by the throat and jumped on his chest,' Ossie answered, 'till he couldn't hardly breathe. He had to run for his life.'

'Cor!' said Benny.

'Some ghosts are a noisy lot, screaming and hollering and rattling chains about. But not him.'

Benny looked about fearfully. 'If a ghost screamed at me, I'd take off.'

'It's mainly the English ones that do that,' Ossie said reassuringly. 'Australian ghosts are mainly pretty quiet.'

Benny fidgeted. 'This one might be a German ghost. All the people around here came out from Germany. Kreutzer did.'

'That's what I'm saying,' Ossie answered.

'German ghosts are a quiet lot too. Except for the poltergeists.'

'Poltergeists?'

'Yes, poltergeists. They're the ones that throw things about.'

'Cor, I don't think I like them either,' Benny said.

'They knock stuff off the shelves and that. Pick things up and take a shot at you behind your back.'

'Jeepers!'

'And they can see in the dark.'

'I hate poltergeists,' Benny said firmly. 'They're the worst of the lot, I reckon.'

'You can't see 'em, that's the trouble,' Ossie said. 'Some people reckon they're black, like the darkness, and that's why.'

'Poltergeists are the worst,' Benny said earnestly.

'Most ghosts are white.' Ossie spoke with clear conviction.

'Are they?'

'Most ghosts.'

'They're not so scarey, white ghosts.'

'They still scare the daylights out of you,' Ossie said, 'but at least you can see what you're up against.'

'They'd still scare me,' Benny said, nodding his head wholeheartedly. 'I wouldn't like any colour of ghost, not after Maria Rollenberg. She frightened the tripe out of me.'

A few weeks later Benny's cousin, Arthur, came up from Adelaide to stay on Uncle Gus's farm for a week. Benny disliked him. He had big feet, big ears and an even bigger mouth. He knew everything and he laughed and jeered at the idea of ghosts. Benny felt hemmed in by him, tongue-tied and depressed.

They were out in the stables on the second day, the two of them, and Arthur was rolling all over the place with laughter because Benny had mentioned that Uncle Gus had heard ghostly footsteps on the Bethel road.

Benny detested Arthur more and more. How could he even begin to talk to him? A know-all who didn't know anything, who couldn't even imagine what it was like to be out alone on the ranges in the darkness before dawn, to feel the touch of starlight on his hands, the dark breeze on his cheeks, the witching interplay of moonlight and shadow under the tall trees by the road, the deformed yacca rearing up suddenly at his side in the gloom like an inquisitive gooseneck, the touch of a rabbit's fur in the cold of a winter's morning, the magic of a still dam shining in the darkness like a patch of night sky surprised in a valley, the sound that was almost the sound of breathing on the loneliness of the hills, the unheard footsteps on the Bethel road, the unseen speed of poltergeists. . . . How could he, Benny, ever talk to someone like Arthur?

'And as for Uncle Gus and the ghostly footsteps on the road,' Arthur was saying, 'really you have to be joking. How many drunks hear pink elephants stomping around every night of the week!'

Benny was getting too angry and too tired to argue any more, but he felt that he should throw out at least one last challenge.

'What about the ghost of Maria Rollenberg?' he asked fiercely. 'Dozens of people have seen her, and so have I.'

Arthur laughed and slapped him on the shoulder. 'Do you believe everything you see, Ben? What about the bloke who saws a lady in half at the show

– all without blood?' He paused because he reckoned he had Benny reeling. 'Optical illusion, Ben! You think you see something, but it's really something quite different. Like flying saucers.'

'That wasn't a flying saucer,' Benny said stubbornly. 'It was a galloping ghost.'

Arthur rolled about in agonies of delight at that. 'Galloping ghosts is about right, Ben. A patch of moonlight cantering along between two clouds, or car headlights reflected from something a long way away, like a window or a mirror; that's how you make ghosts in the night.'

Benny was inwardly exhausted. He was in such a state of rage and frustration and conflict that he felt he either had to punch Arthur very hard in the stomach or burst into tears and fling himself down with his face pressed into the old saddle rugs by the door of the stable where they were standing.

Luckily Ossie came up just at that moment. Benny was so relieved that he almost flung himself on his shoulder instead, which would have shocked Ossie to the bone.

'Benny! Hey, Benny!' Ossie was leaning forward with the haste of his walking – a sure sign of important news. He was about to pour it all out to Benny when he spied Arthur standing in the doorway. He stopped short, recognising him from previous visits.

'Good day.'

'Good afternoon, Oscar.'

'Up for a holiday?'

'Yes, for one week of the vacation.'

'Having a good time?'

'I've only just arrived. I've been talking to Ben, telling him how ridiculous all these ghost stories are.'

'Pretty stupid are they, d'you reckon?'

'Ludicrous.'

They were all silent for a while. It would have been a difficult time if Arthur hadn't been called inside just then, leaving Ossie and Benny alone.

'What a creep!' Benny said.

'He's a real squirt, ain't he?' Ossie agreed. But then he remembered his news and forgot all about Arthur in the excitement of it. 'Hey, Benny,' he said, lowering his voice conspiratorially in case the shed's ears were listening, 'd'you know what old Kronkie's got on the notice in his window?' Kronkie was Mr Eddie Kronk, butcher, of Kapunda, who paid Benny twenty cents a pair for his rabbit carcasses and put up all kinds of clever slogans such as 'Pleasant Meating', and 'From Meat to You', to attract more customers.

Benny looked at Ossie excitedly. He could tell from his friend's face that he was the bearer of big news. 'No. What?'

Ossie gloated. 'He wants pigeons. As many as he can get.'

'Pigeons?'

'Pigeons. That's what it says on the notice.'

Benny was deflated. 'What's he want pigeons for?'

Ossie sensed Benny's disappointment and was ready with the facts. 'I asked him that.'

'What did he say?'

'Squobbin aspic.'

Benny wrinkled up his face in disgust. 'Squobbin aspic? What's that supposed to mean?'

Ossie was just as mystified as Benny was. 'I don't know. Maybe it's the name of the bloke down in Adelaide that he's going to sell 'em to.'

'Sounds a snotty sort of name. Are you sure it wasn't squabblin'?'

'Could've been.' Ossie dismissed the finer points of the words as irrelevant. 'Anyway, it doesn't matter. The important thing is that he's willing to pay fifty cents a pair.'

Benny nearly fell over the hitching rail near the stable door. 'Fifty cents! Holy crackers!'

Ossie was grinning far back around the sides of his head like a happy hippopotamus. 'That's right. I checked twice, to make sure.'

'Why's he paying so much?' Benny asked suspiciously. 'The old goanna only pays me twenty cents for rabbits.'

Ossie shrugged. 'It's for the Gourmets, he said.'

'Gourmets? Who the heck are they?'

'Don't know. But that's what old Kronkie said.'

Benny puzzled with the name and tasted it on his tongue. 'Must be a religious crowd – like the Catholics. Maybe they only eat pigeons on Fridays, or something. They must be pretty keen if they're willing to pay that much for pigeons.'

Ossie's eyes gleamed above his cheeks like a chubby pig's and his big leathery ears stood out stiff with delight. 'That's why I came straight over,' he said. 'That price might only last for a week.'

Benny eased himself up on to the hitching rail and turned his attention to matters of practical finance. 'How many d'you reckon we can get at your place? Twenty?'

'About that.'

'There wouldn't be more than ten or a dozen around here,' Benny said. 'Too many blooming cats.'

'A dozen's a dozen,' Ossie said profoundly.

Benny was not wildly enthusiastic. 'So we'd get maybe thirty altogether. That's fifteen pairs. Seven or eight dollars.' He considered the point for a second. 'I s'pose it's easier than trapping rabbits.'

'I'll say it is,' Ossie said. 'Just go along the rafters with a torch as soon as it gets dark and lift 'em straight off into a bag. Like picking peaches.'

'It is easier than rabbits,' Benny admitted.

''Course it is,' said Ossie. 'Only takes a few seconds. Four or five a minute, easy. Twenty-five cents a time.'

Benny's eyes were beginning to shine too. 'A dollar a minute,' he said. 'I wish there were more pigeons.'

Ossie looked about furtively to make sure that nobody was watching or listening. 'I know where we can get more,' he said softly. 'Hundreds and hundreds more.'

Benny sensed something suspicious and clandestine in Ossie's manner and edged back a little. 'You're not going to pinch 'em, Ossie?'

Ossie kept on smiling idiotically and shook his head vigorously. 'No. Everything's above board. I've even got proper permission to take 'em.'

Benny was nonplussed. 'Hundreds of 'em?' he repeated.

'Hundreds,' replied Ossie.

'I give up. Where?'

Ossie's eyes were suddenly dark and piercing; he was breathing in a suppressed kind of way.

'*Gartenschmuck!*'

Benny shot up off the hitching rail as if he'd been stuck by the upthrust point of a bag needle. '*Gartenschmuck?*'

Ossie was eager and wide-eyed. 'What d'you say?'

Benny was aghast. 'You must be off your crumpet. *Gartenschmuck!* In the *night!*'

'It would only be early dark. Straight after sundown.'

'No thanks! Not any sort of dark. Not in that place.'

'I'll bet it's not half as bad as everyone says.'

'Half of Maria Rollenberg is more than I can take,' said Benny. 'Even a quarter of a ghost would put the wind up me.'

Ossie tried a different line. 'The Richter boys are always working around the place – in the stables and sheep-yards and that. They never see anything.'

'Yes,' Benny answered. 'In the *day*-time!'

'Well, the early evening is nearly the day-time.'

'Except that it's dark,' Benny said ironically; 'it's a sort of dark day-time.'

Ossie persevered. 'I watched it all day, nearly, through Dad's telescope, and it was just as calm as your place is.'

'That's not too calm with Uncle Gus around.'

'The Richter boys were crutching and drafting. They had their horses there, and the dogs were running around as happy as Larry. That's when I went over and asked about the pigeons.'

'What did they say?'

'Glad to get rid of 'em. Ought to pay us a bounty, Herbie said, just to clean 'em out. Like a plague they are, scratching out the seed, mucking up the water troughs, playing up hell's delight.'

Benny was far from converted. 'What did they say about . . . about the place being haunted?'

'Nothing. Just asked if we were game, that's all.'

'There you are,' said Benny. 'They were having you on.'

'No they weren't. They want us to take the pigeons. Honest.'

'Why don't *they* take 'em. You never see them there after dark.'

'No reason to. They got more money than they know what to do with.'

The mention of money brought avarice back into Ossie's eyes. He stepped forward and took Benny eagerly by the sleeve. 'Listen, Ben, you should've seen the pigeons that were there, even in the day-time. The place was crawling with them. They've been nesting and breeding there for donkey's years and nobody's ever disturbed them. They're all over the stables and everywhere – on the rafters, in the straw thatch of the old sheds, on top of the posts, in the forks of the uprights, even in the house.'

'I'm not going in there,' Benny said quickly, back-ing away from Ossie. 'Not in the old house.'

'We won't have to,' Ossie answered persuasively. 'There's a fortune in the sheds.'

Benny laughed wryly. 'You're always on about fortunes, Os.'

'It *is* a fortune, Benny – for blokes like you and me. I reckon we could get four hundred pigeons from over there in a couple of nights. Two hundred each. And that's a hundred dollars.'

'A hundred dollars!'

'Work it out for yourself.' Ossie paused and looked at Benny cunningly. 'You could have your motor-bike even before you could get a licence, nearly.'

It was clear that Benny was wavering. 'You reckon there are that many? Honest?'

Ossie swept his arms around like a tycoon gloating over his estate. 'It's just a start. We could get

a thousand pairs if we wanted to. Five hundred
dollars.'

That was too much for Benny. 'Jeepers. Five
hundred dollars!'

'We'll never get another chance like it, I'll tell you
that.'

Benny seemed to take a deep breath. 'All right, I'll
come.'

'Cock of the heap, old rooster!' said Ossie exult-
ingly. 'I knew you would.'

'When?' said Benny uncertainly. 'Not . . . not
tonight?'

'No, we'll do ours and yours tonight. Just to get our
hands in. Then tomorrow night we'll have a crack at
the big money.' He was so excited by his own enthusiasm that he ran around in a circle plucking
imaginary pigeons down from the rails and posts.
'*Gartenschmuck*,' he chanted, making a kissing noise
with his lips, 'we love you, *Gartenschmuck; Schmuck!*
Schmuck! Schmuck!'

While he was watching Ossie's money-dance
Benny had a sudden thought. 'Hey,' he said, 'what
about Arthur?'

Ossie stopped short for a split second and then
went on dancing and catching airy pigeons. 'We'll
take him with us,' he said.

'What? That toad?'

'He'll be useful. Fetch and carry. Hold things. Lug
the stepladder around and tie up the bags.' Ossie
paused. 'And if we meet a nasty we'll push him out in
front.' He tittered gleefully. 'Maybe a poltergeist'll
twist his ears off.'

But Benny was never one to invite the anger of the
spirits. 'You can talk,' he said soberly. 'If a poltergeist gets hold of your ears, Ossie, you'll be done for.'

All the arrangements went smoothly. To Benny's surprise nobody objected to his idea of adding a little pigeon-catching to his rabbit-trapping enterprises. Uncle Gus even applauded it. 'Very goot,' he said warmly. 'Pigeons do not'ing but *Dreck-Dreck-Dreck* all over d' place. On d' saddles, on d' rugs, on your head even. Best to screw dere necks.'

Of course Benny didn't say anything about *Gartenschmuck*. They didn't tell Arthur either, because they knew he would go clacking all over the place with the news. They just said they were going pigeon-catching for the next two or three nights to help butcher Kronk with supplies for the Gourmets. The first night went brilliantly. The pigeons seemed to sit mesmerised on the rafters in the beam of the torch, and all the boys had to do was pick them off and pop them into the big bags that Arthur held ready. It was just as Ossie had predicted. When they'd cleaned out Uncle Gus's sheds they went over to Ossie's place and did the same thing there. It was incredible. In less than two hours they had more than forty – almost without effort.

'Ten dollars,' Ossie said, gloating. 'It's money for jam.'

'Is it ever,' said Benny. 'Ding-a-ling-a-ling!'

Ossie's eyes were shining. 'Wait till tomorrow night. We'll be millionaires.'

Even Arthur seemed mildly interested – not because of the money, which he said was peanuts, but because of the adventure of it all. Skulking about in old sheds at night, pin-pointing the quarry, seizing it quietly and firmly without any fuss, and then popping it into a big bag like a safe-breaker's loot – it was a new and unusual experience. He was buoyed up, too, by Ossie's praise.

'Good on you, Arthur,' Ossie said loudly and exuberantly when the bag closed over another victim. 'You're worth your weight in pigeon droppings!'

'Where are we going tomorrow night?' Arthur asked.

'We'll find some more spots,' Ossie answered vaguely. 'I'll call for you and Benny just after sundown.'

And so the *Gartenschmuck* adventure began. They set out in the twilight, walking quickly down the Nagala Creek and then skirting the outriders of the range until they came to the knoll that looked down on the old homestead. Arthur held the bags and Ossie and Benny carried the light stepladder between them. The gloom had deepened, but there was just enough light still left in the sky to throw up the silhouettes of the ridges and the outlines of the farm buildings that were clustered in the valley below the house. Their size astounded Benny – stables, sheds, barns, tanks, sties, and mustering yards – all grouped around a central keep that looked like the sheltered market-place of an ancient village; and beyond it stood the house, a dark monstrous shape in the darkness.

'Cor,' said Benny in an unnecessary whisper, 'big, ain't it?'

'Huge,' Ossie answered in a subdued voice. 'No wonder it gives people the creeps.'

Benny's enthusiasm for pigeon-hunting was ebbing fairly quickly. 'D'you think . . . d'you think we'll be able to find our way?' he asked.

Even Arthur was hushed and tense. 'D'you mean nobody lives there at all?' he asked.

'Only ghosts,' said Ossie without thinking, and

then wished he hadn't said it because it set all three of them on edge.

Arthur was the first to put on some front again. 'There are no such things so the place must be empty.'

'Sure,' said Ossie. 'Except for pigeons. Millions of 'em. We'll make a fortune tonight, I tell you.'

Arthur was clutching the empty bags. 'How are we going to carry them all back?'

'What we can't carry we'll leave and pick up tomorrow.' Ossie moved forward. 'Come on, down this track. Better lift your big feet.'

They filed down silently to the valley floor and moved forward through the darkness to the first group of stables. Ossie was a born leader and he had spied out the land carefully beforehand. 'This way,' he whispered cautiously. 'They ought to be thick in here.' It was a huge horse-stable, sixty or seventy metres long, fitted with dozens of stalls and a feed trough like a wooden canal that ran from one end to the other. Ossie flashed the torch briefly along the rafters and cross-struts. There were pigeons everywhere, bunched up in long lines like starlings on a fence.

'Look at 'em,' Ossie whispered fiercely and greedily. 'Like beads on a string.'

He switched off the torch and for a second or two they couldn't see a thing until their eyes adjusted to the darkness again. Arthur blundered into the step-ladder and reeled back against Ossie.

'Watch it! Watch it!' Ossie hissed. 'We don't want to let every flaming thing know that we're here.'

'What thing?' Benny asked nervously.

Ossie ignored him. 'Come on, this way. We'll start from one end and work down.' He was jubilant at the certainty of the catch. 'It'll be like taking cobs off the corn.'

'You mean corn off the cob,' said Arthur.

'All right, Einstein,' Ossie answered tartly. 'I mean peas in a pot.'

'That's dirty,' said Benny. 'You mean peas in a pod.'

'That's what I said! Now stop clowning, you two, and get this ladder up there.'

They pushed and manoeuvred for a moment. 'That's it. Now, Arthur, ready with the bag. Benny, you steady the steps.' And Ossie climbed up lightly for the first assault on their unsuspecting prey.

For half an hour they worked stealthily and efficiently, taking it in turns to stand at the top of the stepladder seizing the pigeons. By now their routine was well established. The light-beam flashed on to the roosting bird, two hands closed over its body firmly and evenly to prevent any struggling or the noisy flapping of wings, the neck of the bag opened momentarily to admit the new victim and then closed tightly again after it.

'Good work,' whispered Ossie as they made the fiftieth capture. 'Benny, you're deadly with that torch. Laser Ben, they call him.'

They moved the ladder stealthily as they worked their way down the stable. 'Better not put too many in one bag,' Benny said. 'It's cruel, and they might die.'

'I've used three already,' Arthur answered. 'We're going to run out of bags.'

'Then we'll lock up the ones we can't take and come back for them in the morning.'

'Where are you going to lock 'em up?' asked Benny. 'In the dunny?'

'We'll find a room or a bit of a barn somewhere.

We're not stopping this bonanza just because we haven't got anything to put them in.'

When they had cleaned out the stable as well as they could they moved on to the old cowshed and dairy next door. Here they were less successful. The building was far more decrepit, with tumbledown walls and debris all over the floor, and the pigeons seemed wilier and more restless. Twice Arthur missed one altogether and it went flying off frantically into the night; once Ossie himself let one wrench its wings free and it filled the night with feathers and flapping; and once Benny would have capsized the ladder altogether if Ossie hadn't lunged forward to brace it at the last minute.

'Careful! Careful!' he hissed urgently. 'Hell's teeth, do you want to crack open your melon?'

Benny came down, crestfallen. 'I reckon it's time we packed up, Os.'

Ossie looked up, as if to consult the sun. 'What's the time?'

'I don't know,' Arthur answered. 'We've been here a good while.'

'How long?'

'A few hours. Longer, maybe.'

'Easy, I reckon,' Benny said.

Ossie wiped his forehead to get rid of dust and feathers rather than perspiration. 'It's later than I thought, then. We'd better get back or everyone will be wondering where the heck we are.'

'Come on, then.' Benny was all for retreating while things were still going well.

'What about the pigeons?' Arthur asked. 'We can't possibly carry all these.'

'How many have we got?' Benny said.

Ossie shone the torch on the bulging sacks.

'Couple of hundred, near enough. Fifty dollars' worth.' He swept the beam around lavishly. 'And we've hardly touched the surface. We can keep this going for a week.' Benny pointed to the sacks. 'We can't carry 'em in those things,' he said, 'not as many as that. They'd die, half of them.'

'We'll have to leave some here, and come back for them in the morning,' said Ossie. 'Better look around for something to put them in.'

They were about to move out to search the other sheds when a faint gust of wind moved over them momentarily and the night was suddenly filled with stealthy sounds – not only the secret creaking of timber and the rustling of thatch, but the darkness itself moving like a hushed tide, a mysterious breathing amid the desolate buildings.

Another gust came and went, and this time a low note moaned faintly with it and was gone again – a muted windwail, perhaps, or a human being mourning privately and desperately in the inner recesses of the old house. It stung the boys like ice.

'What . . . what was that?' Benny asked, cold goose pimples pricking his neck.

'Put out that torch!' Ossie whispered to Arthur. 'Listen!'

They waited motionless, holding their breaths. But there was nothing more.

'Only the wind,' murmured Ossie at last.

'I . . . I think we ought to go,' Benny whispered.

'What, and leave all the pigeons in the bags?'

'I reckon there's . . . something, something else besides us around here.' Benny's forebodings were enough to set all three of them trembling again, including Arthur who seemed to have dropped his former bravado like a pair of wet pants.

'Enough of that talk, Benny,' Ossie hissed. 'You give a bloke the creeps.'

They were huddling together in the darkness, touching one another for the comfort of human contact. Suddenly they caught their breaths again and a little thrill of terror swept each one; for a low moan rose and fell once more, and faded into a sigh, into a kind of rustle like the movement of huge mothwings in the gloom. Benny's hair stood up as stiff as sticks.

'It's . . . it's M . . . M . . . Maria R . . . Rollenberg,' he said in a hushed whisper. 'I told you we should have made a run for it.'

'How . . . how d'you know it's her?'

'That's the way she sounds. Uncle Gus has heard it lots of times.'

Ossie turned to Arthur. 'Give us the torch, Arthur,' he whispered. 'You're shaking so much you're rattling the batteries.'

'She's t . . . tall and white,' Benny went on, 'd . . . dressed like a bride.'

They waited tensely. 'To meet her would be bad enough, but Kreutzer'd be worse.'

'Who's K . . . Kreutzer?' asked Arthur in a strangled sort of croak.

'The bridegroom. They reckon he murdered her and then killed himself. They were never seen again.'

'L . . . let's go, Oscar,' Arthur pleaded in a wheedling tone.

'I'm . . . I'm going, Os,' whispered Benny. 'You coming or not?'

'All right,' Ossie whispered back, rather relieved that the decision had been taken out of his hands, 'but don't blame me if we lose half the pigeons.'

'Which way?' asked Arthur.

'Round here; careful!'

They were up near the far end of the dairy. To reach the track down the valley they either had to retrace their steps through the cowshed and horse-stables, or take a short cut across the central court-yard surrounded by the other buildings. Ossie decided on the short cut.

They moved out cautiously into the open air, hold-ing on to one another. It was very dark now. A milky moonstain was travelling fast behind the banks of clouds, but it was so erratic and so hidden that it gave no light. If anything, it emphasised the darkness instead. 'Mind your feet,' Ossie whispered. 'And keep close together.' There was no need to give the warning because Benny and Arthur were treading on his heels, fearful that at any minute they would feel a clammy grip and find themselves walking hand in hand with something from beyond the grave. Ossie groped his way along the outside wall of the dairy towards the courtyard, leaving the drafting yards, sties, breeding pens, and old smokehouse on his left. The wall was high   six or seven metres at least – because it formed part of the loft and barn beyond. Even in the thick darkness Ossie felt dwarfed by it. Then he reached the gap where a gate had once led into the yard, passed through it, and turned sharply left. Benny and Arthur followed.

And there it was! Rearing up in the air before them. More horrible than anything in life or death – evil and silent and ghostly. And so close to them that they could have touched it. It was huge. Three metres high at least, floating a metre above the ground, towering above them with its arms stretched upwards and outwards as if crucified to the night, its head faceless; its torso white and wraith-like.

Yet unmistakably a body, a form. A supernatural being.

After the first blood-chilling shock, the gurgling *Ar-r-r-k* from Ossie and the thump of the torch falling from his hands, they stood frozen for a part-second, their hearts seemingly no longer beating, their blood frigid, their eyes starting from their sockets. The monstrous apparition sensed their presence and turned towards them.

And then they fled. Screaming. Back through the open gateway, back past the wall of the dairy, the tumbledown cowshed, falling and stumbling, colliding into one another, crying out for help, catching up and being left behind, stampeding, never looking back, feeling the monstrous pursuit, the evil presence breathing close, the chill clutch at their shoulders, running on and on, straining away from the sheds and buildings, the diabolic house, the cursed boundaries of *Gartenschmuck*. Fleeing, fleeing, fleeing.

By a miracle they kept together in the end, guided by their panting cries and their wheezing, and the shapes of their silhouettes as they reached the top of the knoll at the head of the valley. And there, for the first time, they looked back, and paused and finally sank down on the grass exhausted, speechless, shattered, with bloodied knees and heaving chests, and minds too shaken even to comprehend.

'Jesus!' said Ossie, sincerely and piously. 'Dear Lord God Jesus!'

Arthur was lying on his elbows, sobbing, trying to get his breath back. Benny was crying from shock.

'Oh God!' Ossie repeated, panting desperately, 'Oh God!'

They lay there wheezing and retching for a long while.

'Did . . . did you get . . . get a look at it?' Ossie asked at last.

A shudder seemed to well up from the soles of Benny's boots and swept over him so violently that his whole body shook. 'Ur-r-r-r-r-gh! Horrible! Horrible! Horrible!'

'It was . . . was a . . . a . . . ghost!' Arthur said at last.

Ossie shuddered too. 'Gr-r-r-rh! And so close I could have touched the stinking thing.'

'A real ghost,' Arthur repeated, as if still unwilling to believe it.

'And not . . . not Maria Rollenberg,' wheezed Benny. 'So . . . it . . . it must've been . . . Kreutzer. Guarding the place.'

Ossie roused himself then and crawled up on to his hands and knees. 'We'd better keep going,' he said, looking back fearfully towards *Gartenschmuck*, 'before it decides to come after us.'

Arthur agreed. 'Better hurry.'

Benny was rummaging about with the inside seams of his trouser legs.

Ossie stood up. 'Come on, Benny! What are you hassling about with down there?'

'Well that's the last straw,' said Benny. 'I've wet my pants.'

Who's a Pretty Boy, Then?

Jan Mark

Rachel's house had a very small garden. The people on the end of the terrace had a big one, round the side as well as at the back, but Rachel's house was in the middle, so there was only a small strip of garden behind, and none at all in front. Once Rachel had travelled right to the top of Debenham's, on the escalators, to where they kept all the furniture and carpets. Some of the carpets were laid out on the floor, as if they were in a real house, and there was one carpet that was as big as Rachel's whole garden; well, almost. Two of those carpets would definitely have been bigger than Rachel's garden.

Rachel's mum could have done with a bit more room because she liked growing things, and there was not much scope for gardening on a carpet, but she made the most of what space there was. Along the back fence, by the alley, there were sprouts and cabbages, with fringes of radishes and spring onions in between, and the lusty rhubarb that was trying to get out, through the palings. In the middle was a grass plot that had to be cut with shears because there wasn't enough to buy a mower for, and down either side were flowers. Mum even had little bushes growing in old buckets, on the concrete up by the back door, and there was a stringy sort of vine that did not look at all well, and that had come over the wall from Mrs Sergeant's.

'For a bit of peace,' said Mum, pruning it tenderly. So the whole garden was a carpet of grass and plants except for one threadbare patch, the size of a large hearthrug, right next to the house. Nothing grew there.

Mum couldn't understand it. It was a good sunny spot, sheltered from the wind, but it made no difference what she planted, nothing came up. She tried carrots and lettuce first, and when they failed she put in onions, then beetroot, then marrows and finally nasturtiums which are difficult *not* to grow, but by now it was getting late in the year, and nothing was growing anywhere. Next spring she set bedding plants instead of seeds, but after a few days the plants looked poorly and lay down limp. Then she got silly and planted dandelions. 'They'll grow if nothing else does,' she said, but they didn't. Even fireweed would not grow there.

'It must be the drains,' Gran said. 'You ought to get the council to have a look. It might be typhoid.'

'I'd have thought bad drains would be good for plants,' said Mum. 'Ever see a carrot with typhoid?' Gran sniffed.

By the time they had lived in the house for three years Rachel's little sister Donna had been born, Gran had moved to Maidstone, Rachel was at the Junior school and Dad suddenly started to be interested in budgerigars. Gran had kept a blue

budgerigar called Pip in a cage on the sideboard, but
Dad did not approve of birds like that.

'Is it cruel to keep them in cages then?' Rachel
asked. She thought it probably was cruel.

'I don't know about cruel,' said Dad, 'but it
doesn't look natural to me, a full-grown bird standing on one leg with a bell on its head saying, "Who's a
pretty boy, then?"' and kissing itself in the mirror. If
we have any birds they're going to behave like birds';
and on the bald patch where nothing grew, he built
an aviary.

First he put down concrete, and over this went a
tall enclosure of wire netting on a frame of battens, in
the angle of the house and the garden wall. At one
end was a wooden sentry box with perches, where the
birds could sleep safe from draughts and passing
rats.

'There aren't any rats round here,' said Mum.

'Livestock attracts them,' said Dad, and made all
the joints and angles rat-proof. Rachel hoped there
would be rats.

At the weekend Dad and Rachel took the bus out
past the M2 flyover and spent the afternoon looking
in the woods for good sound branches so that the
birds would have somewhere to sit, like wild birds,
and afterwards they went up on to the downs to find
lumps of chalk, essential for healthy feathers. They
had a bit of trouble on the way home with what the
bus conductor referred to as half a dead tree. 'I
ought to sell you a ticket for it,' he said, and there
was some unpleasantness with a woman who complained that Dad had tried to put her eye out, but
they brought it home safely and it was set up in the
flight, which was what Dad called the open part of
the aviary.

'Why's it called an aviary, Dad?' Rachel asked.

'Look it up,' said Dad, as he always did when Rachel wanted to know what words meant. She was never sure whether this was because he thought it was good for her to look things up, or because he did not know the answer. She took care not to ask him which it was. This time she fetched the dictionary and learned that the Latin word for bird was *avis*. She was pleased to know some Latin.

For a long time the dictionary had been the only book on the shelf, but now it had been joined by magazines and illustrated books about budgerigars. The birds in the pictures were brightly coloured and when Rachel leafed through the pages her eye was captured by succulent names; Lutinos, Opalines and Satinettes, Cobalts, Cinnamons and Visual Violets; glassy, glossy words with rare flavours. She imagined the dead branch in the aviary brilliant with expensive sweets like a fabulous Christmas tree.

Then the budgerigars arrived. There were six of them and they came in little cardboard boxes with holes in the sides. Dad took them into the aviary and let them loose; then he left, without the birds following him, because he had built the aviary with double doors. There was a space between them which was, he said, the air-lock. Rachel looked up air-lock and decided that he must be joking.

'What are we going to call them?' Rachel said.

'We're not going to call them anything,' Dad said. 'They don't need names. And another thing,' he said, sternly, to Rachel and Mum and Donna who had come out to watch, 'I don't want anyone trying to teach them to talk. These budgerigars are going to be as near wild as tame birds can be. There's going to be trouble if I catch any of them creeping up to me and saying, "Who's a pretty boy, then?" And no wolf-whistles.'

Mum went indoors to give Donna her lunch, but Rachel stayed close up against the wire and watched the budgerigars ('I don't want to hear anyone calling them budgies') exploring their new home, bouncing on the branches and tidying their feathers, investigating seed trays, grit pans and water pots. There was no doubt that they looked much more impressive in their aviary than Pip had done in his cage, but she could not help wondering if they wouldn't be happier with a bell or two, and a mirror.

'They don't need mirrors,' said Dad, 'they've got each other to look at.'

When the birds had settled in they began to purr and chirrup in the sunshine.

'See,' said Dad, 'they can talk to each other. There's no point in making them learn words, those squawks are all the language they need. They mean something.'

'So do words,' Rachel said.

'Not to budgerigars,' Dad said, firmly. 'You can teach a budgerigar to say the Lord's Prayer. You can teach him to sing *God Save the Queen*. You can teach him to count to a hundred backwards, but he'll never know what he's saying. They don't really *talk*, they just copy sounds.'

Rachel remembered Pip, looking sideways into his mirror and saying coyly, 'Who's a pretty boy, then?' He had always sounded as though he knew exactly what it meant, and very pleased with himself; but then, budgerigars usually did sound pleased with themselves, and they looked smug, too. Rachel thought it might be something to do with having no neck.

It was a fine warm August, that year. Donna sat in her pram in the middle of the grass, and squawked when the birds squawked. She would watch them for hours as they bowed and curtseyed, turned somer-saults and hung by one leg. Rachel liked spying on them when they went to sleep in the shelter, with their heads turned right round and their beaks buried in their back feathers. It gave her a furry feeling in her front teeth; little kittens had the same effect, and baby rabbits.

The budgerigars had been in residence for almost six weeks when Dad came home from work one evening in a bad mood. They could tell he was in a bad mood by the way he shut the kitchen door. He always came in through the back gate and paused to have a look at the birds on his way past the aviary, before coming indoors. Tonight he didn't stop in the kitchen; he went straight through to the front room where Rachel and Mum were watching television.

'Own up, then,' he said. 'Who did it?'

'Who did what?' said Mum. 'Keep your voice down or we shall have old mother Sergeant banging on the wall.'

'Who's been at those birds?'

Mrs Sergeant thumped on the wall.

'Have they got out, then?' Mum looked alarmed. 'Rachel, have you been fiddling . . .?'

'Oh, they're all there,' said Dad, '*and one of them's talking*. Who did it?'

'What did it say?' Rachel asked. She hoped that it had not said hello. She always said it herself as she passed the aviary on her way to school; not to teach them, just to be friendly.

'I say "Good morning, ladies and gentlebirds" when I put the seed in,' Mum said. Rachel was surprised. It was not the kind of joke that Mum went in for. 'Don't tell me that *they've* been saying "Good morning, ladies and gentlebirds" too,' said Mum.

'Stop acting innocent,' said Dad. 'Come out here and listen.'

They went out to the aviary. One of the birds was white, more noticeable than the others and more sociable. Rachel thought of it as Snowball, although she was careful never to say so. When the white bird saw the family standing round, it flew up to a branch and sidled along, until it was close to the wire.

'Pretty me,' it said.

'Hear that?' Dad demanded. 'Pretty me! I'll give it pretty me. Who's been saying "Pretty me" to that bird?'

'No,' said Rachel. 'I haven't.' She was not quite sure if this was, in fact, what the bird had said. The words had come out muffled and rather subdued, not at all like Pip's self-satisfied croak. She wished it would speak again but it only sat there on its branch, the little wrinkled eyelids crimping up and down.

'If any of those birds says another word, *one* other word, there'll be trouble,' said Dad. He was looking at Rachel.

'I never,' said Rachel.

'I suppose it was Donna, then.'

Donna hadn't even got around to saying ma-ma yet.

'Well, it wasn't me,' Mum said. 'Why don't you sell up and get canaries instead? They don't have much to say for themselves.' She went indoors.

After tea, when Dad had gone to play darts at the *Man of Kent*, Rachel slipped out to the aviary again. The white bird was still sitting on its twig, next to the wire. Rachel went and stood close, sucking her teeth as Gran used to do with Pip, to indicate that she was ready for a chat. The white bird opened its eyes, and its beak.

'Pity me,' it said, in its sad, hoarse voice. 'Pity me. Pity me.'

Rachel's first thought was, 'Good; it isn't copying anything I've said.' Then she began to wonder who it was copying. Surely no one would deliberately teach a budgerigar to say 'Pity me'? Perhaps Mum had said it without thinking – no; people didn't say things like that without thinking. Perhaps the bird had *tried* to say 'Pretty me' but couldn't talk very well? Perhaps Mrs Sergeant had been having a go at it, over the wall.

Rachel sucked her teeth again.

'Pity me,' said the white bird. One of the green budgerigars, there were two of them, fluttered down from the topmost twig and clung with beak and claws to the wire netting. It turned its head sideways to look at her.

'Pity me,' said the green bird.

The two yellow birds clambered up from below. 'Pity me. Pity me. Pity me.' Rachel shivered. She had not noticed that the sun was down below the roofs of the houses in the next street. The aviary was in shadow and she could only just make out the shape of the blue budgerigar, hunched on its perch in the shelter, in silence, while the white, the green and the yellow birds pressed against the netting and repeated dully, 'Pity me. Pity me.'

The next day was Saturday, mild and still, and in the morning the budgerigars swung and fluttered in the aviary with never a word to say. They nibbled at chickweed, honed their beaks on cuttlefish bones and chucked millet seeds about, very busy being budgerigars; but as the day wore on an uneasy silence settled over the aviary. Birds sang in other gardens but the budgerigars fluffed themselves up, drew their spare feet into their feathers and closed their eyes. They looked, to Rachel, not so much tired as depressed. She went over to the netting, carrying Donna, and said, 'Come on, boys, cheer up.'

A yellow budgerigar opened one eye and said, 'Oh, I'm so cold. Oh, I'm so cold.'

'Pity me,' said the white bird. The others ruffled their feathers and were motionless again.

'Cross my heart,' Rachel gabbled, that evening. 'Cross my heart and cut my throat, it wasn't me.'

'None of that nonsense,' said Dad. 'I want a straight answer, yes or no. Did you or didn't you?'

'No!' Rachel yelled. She was shocked. People didn't yell at Dad. 'I never did. Anyway, if I had, I wouldn't have taught them to say things like that. I'd have taught them "Give us a kiss" and – and—'

'Who's a pretty boy, then?'

'Yes. But I *didn't*.'

It was raining on Sunday. The budgerigars stayed in their shelter and looked at the weather with their small eyes half shut, and said nothing all day. Dad was on late turn the following week, from four till midnight, so he saw the birds only in the daytime when it was bright, and they were bright, but it seemed to Rachel that they were not so bright as they had been, and after Dad left for work, wheeling his bicycle away down the alley, she visited the aviary. The birds, that had stopped flying and gibbering, settled on their twigs and shuffled towards her; all of them, all six. They looked furtive and unwell.

'Pity me,' said the white bird.

'Oh, I'm so cold,' said the two yellow birds.

'Pity me.'

'Cold as clay,' said the blue bird that had never spoken before.

'*What?*'

Rachel jumped and turned round. Mum was standing behind her, lips pressed together tight and frightened.

'What did that bird say?'

'I don't know, Mum.' She did know, but she did not want to tell.

'Don't say anything to your dad. I'm going to watch out, this evening. Someone must be coming into the garden after dark and doing this.'

Mum watched every evening that week, and caught no one, heard nothing, even though she kept up her vigil until Dad came home at midnight. By the weekend the birds had stopped squawking and flying from twig to twig. The chickweed withered untouched; the millet sprays hung neglected from the branches. On Saturday morning Dad and Mum and Rachel stood round the aviary and listened to the listless little voices droning, 'Oh, I'm so cold.' 'Pity me.' 'Oh, I'm so cold.' 'Cold as clay.' 'Pity me. Pity me.'

'This is getting beyond a joke,' Dad said, and talked of calling the police.

'Come off it,' said Mum, 'you can't call the police because your budgies are talking daft.'

'You call that talking daft?'

'No, not really, but they aren't damaged, are they? They haven't been stolen.'

'Not damaged? Look at them.'

They all looked at the bedraggled birds, with their feathers poking out at odd angles like bristles on a bottle brush, and their dreary eyes. The white budgerigar, once the most beautiful of all, had pulled out its tail feathers and slouched on its perch with all the grace of an old shuttlecock.

'What could the police do?' Mum said. 'Question them?'

Dad scowled and went to consult his budgerigar books. Later he went shopping and came home with cod-liver oil and fortified seed and a mineral block like a lump of grey Edinburgh rock.

'To cheer them up,' he said.

'They'd probably fancy a nip of whisky, sooner,' said Mum. 'Wouldn't you?'

They had not cheered up by Sunday evening, and on Monday, the last day of October, Dad was back at work. He was on the night shift now, and did not leave home until twenty to twelve. Rachel heard him go, kept awake by the continual opening and closing all evening of the back door, as Mum and Dad took turns to leap out on the intruder; but they didn't catch anyone. When Dad's rear light had turned left at the end of the alley, Rachel crept downstairs. Mum was clearing up, before going to bed, but she sat down at the table when Rachel padded into the kitchen. She sighed.

'I don't know.'

'I'm sorry, Mum. I couldn't sleep. The back door . . .'

'I didn't mean you, it's those blooming budgies. We've been in and out a dozen times this evening, and we haven't heard anyone.'

'I don't think there's anyone to hear,' said Rachel.

'You get along to bed,' Mum said, crossly. 'You'll be having me see things, next.'

Rachel said, 'I don't think there's anything to see, either. I don't think there's anything at all, and only the birds can hear it. Are you going out to look?'

'No,' said Mum. 'Not on your life – and neither are you.'

When Dad came home from work next morning, he found Mum and Rachel standing by the aviary, watching the budgerigars that drooped on their branches.

'Oh, I'm so cold,' said one.

'I shall always be very cold,' said another, 'cold as clay.'

'I shall always be here,' said a third.

'I shall never go away,' said the white bird.

'Pity me.'

'Pity me.'

'No,' said Dad, for the twentieth time. 'No!' he shouted. 'We are not moving. I never heard such nonsense. We're staying here.'

'Right,' said Mum, 'then it's up to you. Either those birds go or I do.'

The budgerigars were sold to good homes and went to live in cages with bells and mirrors. Donna missed them very much, so instead of the budgerigars they got a Hertz Roller canary that lived up to its name by standing on its toes all day and yelling 'Rrrrrrrrrrrrrrrrrrr' on a very high note. Dad broke up the aviary and on the place where nothing would grow he put down crazy paving in five different cheerful colours with a little pond in the middle. He called it a patio and to decorate it he bought a plastic orange tree in a pot and a plastic stork to stand by the pond. Rachel didn't much like the look of the patio, but the orange tree did not die, and the stork never said a word.

The Strange Illness of Mr Arthur Cook

Philippa Pearce

On a cold, shiny day at the end of winter the Cook family went to look at the house they were likely to buy. Mr and Mrs Cook had viewed it several times before, and had discussed it thoroughly; this was a first visit for their children, Judy and Mike.

Also with the Cooks was Mr Biley, of the house-agent's firm of Ketch, Robb and Biley in Walchester.

'Why's *he* come?' whispered Judy. (And, although the Cooks were not to know this, Mr Biley did not usually accompany clients in order to clinch deals.)

Her parents shushed Judy.

They had driven a little way out of Walchester into the country. The car now turned down a lane which, perhaps fifty years before, had been hardly more than a farm-track. Now there were several houses along it. The lane came to a dead end at a house with a *For Sale* notice at its front gate. On the gate itself was the name of the house: Southcroft.

'There it is!' said Mr Arthur Cook to his two children.

'And very nice, too!' Mr Biley said enthusiastically.

But, in fact, the house was not particularly nice. In size it was small to medium; brick-built, slate-roofed; exactly rectangular; and rather bleak-looking. It stood in the middle of a large garden, also exactly rectangular and rather bleak-looking.

Mike, who tended to like most things that happened to him, said: 'Seems O.K.' He was gazing round not only at the house and its garden, but at the quiet lane – ideal for his bike – and at the surrounding countryside. It would be all far, far better than where they were living now, in Walchester.

Judy, who was older than Mike, and the only one in the family with a sharply pointed, inquisitive nose, said nothing – yet. She looked round alertly, intently.

'Nice big garden for kids to play in,' Mr Biley pointed out.

'I might even grow a few vegetables,' said Mr Cook.

'Oh, Arthur!' his wife said, laughing.

'Well,' Mr Cook said defensively, 'I haven't had much chance up to now, have I?' In Walchester the Cooks had only a paved backyard. But, anyway, Mr Cook, whose job was fixing television aerials on to people's roofs, had always said that in his spare time he wanted to be indoors in an easy chair.

'Anyway,' said Mr Biley, as they went in by the front gate, 'you've lovely soil here. Still in good tilth.'

'Tilth?' said Mr Cook.

'That's it,' said Mr Biley.

They reached the front door. Mr Biley unlocked it, and they all trooped in.

Southcroft had probably been built some time between the two wars. There was nothing antique about it, nor anything of special interest at all. On the other hand, it all appeared to be in good order, even to the house's having been fairly recently redecorated.

The Cooks went everywhere, looked everywhere, their footsteps echoing uncomfortably in empty rooms. They reassembled in the sitting-room, which had french windows letting on to the garden at the back. Tactfully Mr Biley withdrew into the garden to leave the family to private talk.

'Well, there you are,' said Mr Cook. 'Just our size of house. Not remarkable in any way, but snug, I fancy.'

'Remarkable in one way, Arthur,' said his wife. 'Remarkably cheap.'

'A snip,' agreed Mr Cook.

'Why's it so cheap?' asked Judy.

'You ask too many questions beginning with *why*,' said her father, but good-humouredly.

It was true, however, that there seemed no particular reason for the house being as cheap as it was. Odd, perhaps.

'Can't we go into the garden now?' asked Mike.

Mike and Judy went out, and Mr Biley came in again.

There wasn't much for the children to see in the garden. Close to the house grew unkempt grass, with a big old apple tree – the only tree in the garden – which Mike began to climb very thoroughly. The rest of the garden had all been under culti-vation at one time, but now it was neglected, a mess of last season's dead weeds. There were some straggly bushes – raspberry canes, perhaps. There had once been a greenhouse: only the brick founda-tions were left. There was a garden shed, and behind it a mass of stuff which Judy left Mike to investigate. She wanted to get back to the adult conversation.

By the time Judy rejoined the party indoors there was no doubt about it: the Cooks were buying the house. Mr Biley was extremely pleased, Judy noticed. He caught Judy staring at him and jollily, but very unwisely, said: 'Well, young lady?'

Judy, invited thus to join in the conversation, had a great many questions to ask. She knew she wouldn't be allowed to ask them all, and she began almost at random: 'Who used to live here?'

'A family called Cribble,' said Mr Biley. 'A very *nice* family called Cribble.'

'Cribble,' Judy repeated to herself, storing the piece of information away. 'And why—'

At that moment Mike walked in again from the garden. 'There's lots of stuff behind the shed,' he said. 'Rolls and rolls of chicken wire, in an awful mess, and wood – posts and slats and stuff.'

'Easily cleared,' said Mr Biley. 'The previous owners were going to have bred dogs, I believe. They would have erected sheds, enclosures, runs – all that kind of thing.'

'Why did the Cribbles give up the idea?' asked Judy.

Mr Biley looked uneasy. 'Not the Cribbles,' he said, 'the Johnsons. The family here before the Cribbles.'

'Why did the Johnsons give up the idea, then?' asked Judy. 'I mean, when they'd got all the stuff for it?'

'They—' Mr Biley appeared to think deeply, if only momentarily: 'They had to move rather unexpectedly.'

'Why?'

'Family reasons, perhaps?' said Mrs Cook quickly. She knew some people found Judy tiresome.

'Family reasons, no doubt,' Mr Biley agreed.

Judy said thoughtfully to herself: 'The Johnsons didn't stay long enough to start dog-breeding, and they went in such a hurry that they left their stuff behind. The Cribbles came, but they didn't stay long enough to have time to clear away all the Johnsons' stuff. I wonder why *they* left . . .'

Nobody could say that Judy was asking Mr Biley a question, but he answered her all the same. 'My dear young lady,' he said, in a manner so polite as to be also quite rude, 'I do not know why. Nor is it my business.' He sounded as if he did not think it was Judy's either. He turned his back on her and began talking loudly about house-purchase to Mr Cook.

Judy was not put out. She had investigated mysteries and secrets before this and she knew that patience was all-important.

The Cooks bought Southcroft and moved in almost at once. Spring came late that year, and in the continuing cold weather the house proved as snug as one could wish. When the frosts were over, the family did some work outside, getting rid of all the dog-breeding junk: they made a splendid bonfire of the wood, and put the wire out for the dustmen. Mr Cook took a long look at the weeds beginning to sprout everywhere, and groaned. He bought a fork and spade and hoe and rake and put them into the shed.

In their different ways the Cooks were satisfied with the move. The new house was still convenient for Mr Cook's work. Mrs Cook found that the neigh-bours kept themselves to themselves more than she would have liked, but she got a part-time job in a shop in the village, and *that* was all right. Mike made new friends in the new school, and they went riding round the countryside on their bikes. Judy was slower at making friends, because she was absorbed in her own affairs. Particularly in investigation, in which she was disappointed for a time. She could find out so little about the Cribbles and the Johnsons: why they had stayed so briefly at Southcroft, why they had moved in so much haste. The Cribbles now lived the other side of Walchester, rather smartly, in a house with a large garden which they had had expensively landscaped. (Perhaps the size of the garden at Southcroft was what had attracted them to the house in the first place. In the village people said that the Cribbles had already engaged landscape-garden specialists for Southcroft, when they suddenly decided to leave.) As for the Johnsons, Judy discovered that they had moved right away, to Yorkshire, to do their dog-breeding. Before the Cribbles and the Johnsons, an old couple called Baxter had lived in the house for many years, until one had died and the other moved away.

The Cooks had really settled in. Spring brought sunshine and longer days; and it also brought the first symptoms of Mr Cook's strange illness.

At first the trouble seemed to be his eyesight. He complained of a kind of brownish fog between himself and the television screen. He couldn't see clearly enough to enjoy the programmes. He thought he noticed that this fogginess was worse when he was doing daylight viewing, at the weekends or in the early evening. He tried to deal with this by drawing the curtains in the room where the set was on, but the fogginess persisted.

Mr Cook went to the optician to see whether he needed glasses. The optician applied all the usual tests, and said that Mr Cook's vision seemed excellent. Mr Cook said it wasn't – or, at least, sometimes wasn't. The optician said that eyesight could be affected by a person's state of general health, and suggested that, if the trouble continued, Mr Cook should consult a doctor.

Mr Cook was annoyed at the time he had wasted at the optician's, and went home to try to enjoy his favourite Saturday afternoon programme. Not only did he suffer from increased fogginess of vision, but – perhaps as a result, perhaps not – he developed a splitting headache. In the end he switched the set off and went outside and savagely dug in the garden, uprooting ground elder, nettle, twitch and a great number of other weed species. By tea-time he had cleared a large patch, in which Judy at once sowed radishes and mustard and cress.

At the end of an afternoon's digging, the headache had gone. Mr Cook was also able to watch the late night movie on television without discomfort. But his Saturday as a whole had been ruined; and when he went to bed, his sleep was troubled by strange dreams, and on Sunday morning he woke at first light. This had become the pattern of his sleeping recently: haunted dreams and early wakings. On this particular occasion, as often before, he couldn't get to sleep again; and he spent the rest of Sunday – a breezy, sunny day – moving restlessly about indoors from Sunday paper to television set, saying he felt awful.

Mrs Cook said that perhaps he ought to see a doctor, as the optician had advised; Mr Cook shouted at her that he wouldn't.

But, as spring turned to summer, it became clear that something would have to be done. Mr Cook's condition was worsening. He gave up trying to watch television. Regularly he got up at sunrise because he couldn't sleep longer and couldn't even rest in bed. (Sometimes he went out and dug in the garden; and, when he did so, the exertion or the fresh air seemed to make him feel better, at least for the time being.) He lost his appetite; and he was always irritable with his children. He grumbled at Mike for being out so much on his bicycle, and he grumbled at Judy for being at home. Her investigations no longer amused him at all. Judy had pointed out that his illness seemed to vary with the weather: fine days made it worse. She wondered why. Her father said he'd give her *why*, if she weren't careful.

At last Mrs Cook burst out that she could stand this no longer: 'Arthur, you *must* go to the doctor.' As though he had only been waiting for someone to insist, Mr Cook agreed.

The doctor listened carefully to Mr Cook's account of his symptoms and examined him thoroughly. He asked whether he smoked and whether he ate enough roughage. Reassured on both these points, the doctor said he thought Mr Cook's condition might be the result of nervous tension. 'Anything worrying you?' asked the doctor.

'Of course, there is!' exploded Mr Cook. 'I'm ill, aren't I? I'm worried sick about that!'

The doctor asked if there was anything else that Mr Cook worried about: his wife? his children? his job?

'I lie awake in the morning and worry about them all,' said Mr Cook. 'And about that huge garden in that awful state . . .'

'What garden?'

'Our garden. It's huge and it's been let go wild and

I ought to get it in order, I suppose, and – oh, I don't know! I'm no gardener.'

'Perhaps you shouldn't have a garden that size,' suggested the doctor. 'Perhaps you should consider moving into a house with no garden, or at least a really manageable one. Somewhere, say, with just a patio, in Walchester.'

'That's what we moved *from*,' said Mr Cook. 'Less than six months ago.'

'Oh, dear!' said the doctor. He called Mrs Cook into the surgery and suggested that her husband might be suffering from overwork. Mr Cook was struck by the idea; Mrs Cook less so. The doctor suggested a week off, to see what *that* would do.

That week marked the climax of Mr Cook's illness; it drove Mrs Cook nearly out of her wits, and Judy to urgent enquiries.

The week came at the very beginning of June, an ideal month in which to try to recover from overwork. Judy and Mike were at school all day, so that everything was quiet at home for their father. The sun shone, and Mr Cook planned to sit outside in a deckchair and catch up on lost sleep. Then, when the children came home, he would go to bed early with the portable television set. (He assumed that rest would be dealing with fogginess of vision.)

Things did not work out like that at all. During that week Mr Cook was seized with a terrible restlessness. It seemed impossible for him to achieve any repose at all. He tried only once to watch television; and Judy noticed that thereafter he seemed almost – yes, he seemed afraid. He was a shadow of his former self when, at the end of the week, he went back to work.

After he had left the house that morning, Mrs

Cook spoke her fears: 'It'll be the hospital next, I know. And once they begin injecting and cutting up – Oh, why did we ever come to live here!'

'You think it's something to do with the house?' asked Judy. Mike had already set off to school; she lingered.

'Well, your dad was perfectly all right before. I'd say there was something wrong with the drains here, but there's no smell; and, anyway, why should only he fall ill?'

'There is something wrong with the house,' said Judy. 'I couldn't ask the Johnsons about it, so I asked the Cribbles.'

'The Cribbles! That we bought the house from?'

'Yes. They live the other side of Walchester. I went there—'

'Oh, Judy!' said her mother. 'You'll get yourself into trouble with your questions, one of these days.'

'No, I shan't,' said Judy (and she never did). 'I went to ask them about this house. I rang at the front door, and Mrs Cribble answered it. At least, I think it must have been her. She was quite nice. I told her my name, but I don't think she connected me with buying the house from them. Then I asked her about the house, whether *they* had noticed anything.'

'And what did she say?'

'She didn't say anything. She slammed the door in my face.'

'Oh, Judy!' cried Mrs Cook, and burst into tears.

Her mother's tears decided Judy: she would beard Mr Biley himself, of Ketch, Robb and Biley. She was not so innocent as to suppose he would grant her, a child, an official interview. But if she could button-hole him somewhere, she might get from him at least one useful piece of information.

After school that day, Judy presented herself at the offices of Ketch, Robb and Biley in Walchester. She had her deception ready. 'Has my father been in to see Mr Biley yet?' she asked. That sounded respectable. The receptionist said that Mr Biley was talking with a client at present, and that she really couldn't say—

'I'll wait,' said Judy, like a good girl.

Judy waited. She was prepared to wait until the offices shut at half past five, when Mr Biley would surely leave to go home; but much earlier than that, Mr Biley came downstairs with someone who was evidently rather an important client. Mr Biley escorted him to the door, chatting in the jovial way that Judy remembered so well. They said goodbye at the door, and parted, and Mr Biley started back by the way he had come.

Judy caught up with him, laid a hand on his arm: 'Mr Biley – please!'

Mr Biley turned. He did not recognise Judy. He smiled. 'Yes, young lady?'

'We bought Southcroft from the Cribbles,' she began.

Mr Biley's smile vanished instantly. He said, 'I should make clear at once that Ketch, Robb and Biley will not, under any circumstances, handle that property again.'

'Why?' asked Judy. She couldn't help asking.

'The sale of the same property three times in eighteen months may bring income to us, but it does not bring reputation. So I wish you good day.'

Judy said, '*Please*, I only need to ask you one thing, really.' She gripped the cloth of his sleeve. The receptionist had looked up to see what was going on, and Mr Biley was aware of that. 'Well? Be quick,' he said.

'Before the Cribbles and the Johnsons, there were the Baxters: when old Mr Baxter died, where did Mrs Baxter move to?'

'Into Senior House, Waddington Road.' He removed Judy's fingers from his coat-sleeve. 'Remember to tell your father *not* to call in Ketch, Robb and Biley for the resale of the property. Goodbye.'

It was getting late, but Judy thought she should finish the job. She found a telephone box and the right money and rang her mother to say she was calling on Mrs Baxter in the Old People's flats in Waddington Road. She was glad that her telephone-time ran out before her mother could say much in reply.

Then she set off for Waddington Road.

By the time she reached the flats, Judy felt tired, thirsty, hungry. There was no problem about seeing Mrs Baxter. The porter told her the number of Mrs Baxter's flatlet, and said Mrs Baxter would probably be starting her tea. The residents had just finished seeing a film on mountaineering in the Alps, and — as he put it — would be brewing up late.

Judy found the door and knocked. A delicious smell of hot-buttered toast seemed to be coming through the keyhole. A thin little voice told her to come in. And there sat Mrs Baxter behind a teapot with a cosy on it, in the act of spreading honey on a piece of buttered toast.

'Oh,' said Judy, faintly.

Mrs Baxter was delighted to have a visitor. 'Sit down, dear, and I'll get another cup and saucer and plate.'

She was such a nice little old woman, with gingery-grey hair – she wore a gingery dress almost to match – and rather dark pop-eyes. She seemed active, but a bit slow. When she got up in a slow, plump way to get the extra china, Judy was reminded of a hamster she had once had, called Pickles.

Mrs Baxter got the china and some biscuits and poured out another cup of tea. All this without asking Judy her name or her business.

'Sugar?' asked Mrs Baxter.

'Yes, please,' said Judy. 'I'm Judy Cook, Mrs Baxter.'

'Oh, yes? I'll have to get the tin of sugar. I don't take sugar myself, you know.'

She waddled over to some shelves. She had her back to Judy, but Judy could see the little hamster-hands reaching up to a tin marked *Sugar*.

'Mrs Baxter, we live in the house you used to live in: Southcroft.'

The hamster-hands never reached the sugar tin, but stayed up in the air for as long as it might have taken Judy to count ten. It was as though the name Southcroft had turned the little hamster-woman to stone.

Then the hands came down slowly, and Mrs Baxter waddled back to the tea-table. She did not look at Judy; her face was expressionless.

'Have a biscuit?' she said to Judy.

Judy took one. 'Mrs Baxter, I've come to ask you about Southcroft.'

'Don't forget your cup of tea, dear.'

'No, I won't. Mrs Baxter, I must ask you several things—'

'Just a minute dear.'

'Yes?'

'Perhaps you take sugar in your tea?'

'Yes, I do, but it doesn't matter. I'd rather you'd let me ask you—'

'But it does matter,' said Mrs Baxter firmly. 'And I shall get the sugar for you. I don't take it myself, you know.'

Judy had had dreams when she tried to do something and could not because things – the same things – happened over and over again to prevent her. Now she watched Mrs Baxter waddle over to the shelves, watched the little hamster-hands reach up to the sugar-tin and – this time – bring it down and bring it back to the tea-table. Judy sugared her tea, and took another biscuit, and began eating and drinking. She was trying to steady herself and fortify herself for what she now realised was going to be very, very difficult. Mrs Baxter had begun telling her about mountaineering in the Alps. The little voice went on and on, until Judy thought it must wear out.

It paused.

Judy said swiftly: 'Tell me about Southcroft, please. What was it like to live in when you were there? Why is it so awful now?'

'No, dear,' said Mrs Baxter hurriedly. 'I'd rather go on telling you about the Matterhorn.'

'I want to know about Southcroft,' cried Judy.

'No,' said Mrs Baxter. 'I never talk about it. Never. I'll go on about the Matterhorn.'

'Please. You must tell me about Southcroft.' Judy was insisting, but she knew she was being beaten by the soft little woman. She found she was beginning to cry. 'Please, Mrs Baxter. My dad's ill with living there.'

'Oh, no,' cried the little hamster-woman. 'Oh, no, he couldn't be!'

'He is,' said Judy, 'and you won't help!' Stumblingly she began to get up.

'Won't you stay, dear, and hear about the Matterhorn?'

'No!' Judy tried to put her cup back on the dainty tea-table, but couldn't see properly for her tears. China fell, broke, as she turned from the table. She found the handle of the door and let herself out.

'Oh dear, oh dear, oh dear!' the little voice behind her was crying, but whether it was about the broken china or something else it was impossible to say.

Judy ran down the long passages and past the porter, who stared at her tear-wet face. When she got outside, she ran and ran, and then walked and walked. She knew she could have caught a bus home, but she didn't want to. She walked all the way, arriving nearly at dusk, to find her mother waiting anxiously for her. But instead of questioning Judy at once, Mrs Cook drew her into the kitchen, where they were alone. Mike was in the sitting-room, watching a noisy television programme.

Mrs Cook said: 'Your dad telephoned from Walchester soon after you did. He said he wasn't feeling very well, so he's spending the night with your Aunt Edie.'

They stared at each other. Mr Cook detested his sister Edie. 'He'd do anything rather than come here,' said Judy. 'He's afraid.'

Mrs Cook nodded.

'Mum, we'll just have to move from here, for Dad's sake.'

'I don't know that we can, Judy. Selling one house and buying another is very expensive; house-removal is expensive.'

'But if we stay here . . .'

Mrs Cook hesitated; then, 'Judy, what you were doing this afternoon – your calling on old Mrs Baxter – was it any use, any help?'

'No.'

Mrs Cook groaned aloud.

Judy's visit to Mrs Baxter had not led to the answering of any questions; but there was an outcome.

The next day, in the afternoon, Judy and Mike had come home from school and were in the kitchen with their mother. It was a gloomy tea. There was no doubt at all that their father would come home this time – after all, here were his wife and his children that he loved – but the homecoming seemed likely to be a grim and hopeless one.

From the kitchen they heard the click of the front gate. This was far too early to be Mr Cook himself, and, besides, there'd been no sound of a car. Mike, nearest to the window, looked out. 'No one we know,' he reported. 'An old lady.' He laughed to himself. 'She looks like a hamster.'

Judy was at the front door and opening it before Mrs Baxter had had time to ring. She brought her in and introduced her to the others, and Mrs Cook brewed fresh tea while the children made her comfortable in the sitting-room. Besides her handbag, Mrs Baxter was carrying a dumpy zip-up case which seemed heavy; she kept it by her. She was tired. 'Buses!' she murmured.

Mrs Cook brought her a cup of tea.

'Mrs Baxter doesn't take sugar, Mum,' said Judy.

They all sat round Mrs Baxter, trying not to stare at her, waiting for her to speak. She sipped her tea without looking at them.

'Your husband's not very well, I hear,' she said at last to Mrs Cook.

'No.'

'Not home from work yet.'

'Not yet.'

'Mrs Baxter was obviously relieved. She looked at them all now. 'And this is the rest of the family . . .' She smiled timidly at Mike: 'You're the baby of the family?'

Mike said, 'I'm younger than Judy. Mum, if it's OK, I think I'll go out on my bike with Charlie Feather.' He took something to eat and went.

Mrs Baxter said, 'We never had children.'

'A pity,' said Mrs Cook.

'Yes. Everything would be different, if it had been different.' Mrs Baxter paused. 'Do you know, I've never been back to this house – not even to the village – since Mr Baxter died?'

'It was very sad for you,' said Mrs Cook, not knowing what else to say.

'It's been a terrible *worry*,' said Mrs Baxter, as though sadness was not the thing that mattered. Again she paused. Judy could see that she was nerving herself to say something important. She had been brave and resolute to come all this way at all.

Mrs Cook could also see what Judy saw. 'You must be tired out,' she said.

But Judy said gently: 'Why've you come?'

Mrs Baxter tried to speak, couldn't. Instead she opened the zip-up bag and dragged out of it a large, heavy book: *The Vegetable and Fruit Grower's Encyclopaedia and Vade-Mecum*. She pushed it into Mrs Cook's lap. 'It was Mr Baxter's,' she said. 'Give it to your husband. Tell him to use it and work hard in the garden, and I think things will right themselves in time. You need to humour him.'

Mrs Cook was bewildered. She seized upon the last remark: 'I humour him as much as I can, as it is. He's been so unwell.'

Mrs Baxter tittered. 'Good gracious, I didn't mean *your* husband: I meant mine. Humour Mr Baxter.'

'But – but he's dead and gone!'

Mrs Baxter's eyes filled with tears. 'That's just it: he isn't. Not both. He's dead, but not gone. He never meant to go. I knew what he intended; I knew the wickedness of it. I told him – I begged him on his deathbed; but he wouldn't listen. You know that bit of the burial service: "We brought nothing into this world, and it is certain that we can carry nothing out"? Well, there was something he'd dearly have liked to have taken out: he couldn't, so he stayed in this world with it: his garden. We were both good church-goers, but I believe he set his vegetable garden before his God. I know that he set it before me.' She wept afresh.

'Oh, dear, Mrs Baxter!' said Mrs Cook, much distressed.

'When he was dying,' said Mrs Baxter, after she had blown her nose, 'I could see there was something he wanted to say. I'd been reading the twenty-third Psalm to him – you know, about the Valley of the Shadow of Death. He was trying to speak. I leant right over him and he managed to whisper his very last words. He said, "Are the runner beans up yet?" Then he died.'

Nobody spoke. Mrs Baxter recovered herself and went on.

'I knew – I *knew* he wouldn't leave that garden,

after he'd died. I just hoped the next owners would look after it as lovingly as he'd done, and then in time he'd be content to go. That's what I hoped and prayed. But the first lot of people were going to cover it with dog-kennels, and I heard that the second lot were going to lay it out with artificial streams and weeping willows and things. Well, he made their lives a misery, and they left. And now your husband . . .'

'He's just never liked gardening,' said Mrs Cook.

The two women stared at each other bleakly.

'Why can't Dad be allowed to watch telly?' asked Judy. Then, answering herself: 'Oh, I see: he ought to be working in the garden every spare minute in daylight and fine weather.'

'Mr Baxter quite enjoyed some of the gardening programmes, sometimes,' Mrs Baxter said defensively.

There was a long silence.

'It's lovely soil,' said Mrs Baxter persuasively. 'Easy to work. Grows anything. That's why we came to live here, really. All my married life, I never had to buy a single vegetable. Fruit, too – raspberries, strawberries, gooseberries, all colours of currants. So much of everything, for just the two of us, that we had to give a lot of stuff away. We didn't grow plums or pears or apples – except for the Bramleys – because Mr Baxter wouldn't have trees shading the garden. But all those vegetables – you'd find it a great saving, with a family.'

'It seems hard on my husband,' said Mrs Cook.

'It's hard on mine,' said Mrs Baxter. 'Look at him!' Startled Mrs Cook and Judy looked where Mrs Baxter was looking, through the french windows and down the length of the garden. The sun fell on the weedy earth of the garden; on nothing else.

Mrs Cook turned her gaze back into the room, but Judy went on looking, staring until her eyes blurred and her vision was fogged with a kind of brown fogginess that was in the garden. Then suddenly she was afraid.

'But *look*!' said Mrs Baxter, and took Judy's hand in her own little paw that had grown soft and smooth from leisure in Senior House: '*Look!*' Judy looked where she pointed, and the brown fogginess seemed to concentrate itself and shape itself, and there dimly was the shape of an old man dressed in brown from his brown boots to his battered brown hat, with a piece of string tied round the middle of the old brown waterproof he was wearing. He stood in an attitude of dejection at the bottom of the garden, looking at the weeds.

Then Mrs Baxter let go of Judy's hand, and Judy saw him no more.

'That was his garden mac,' said Mrs Baxter. 'He would wear it. When all the buttonholes had gone, as well as the buttons, and I wouldn't repair it any more, then he belted it on with string.'

'He looked so miserable,' said Judy. She had been feeling sorry for her father; now she began to feel sorry for Mr Baxter.

'Yes,' said Mrs Baxter. 'He'd like to go, I've no doubt of it; but he can't leave the garden in that state.' She sighed. She gathered up her handbag and the other empty bag.

'Don't go!' cried Mrs Cook and Judy together.

'What more can I do? I've told you; I've advised you. For *his* sake, too, I've begged you. No, I can't do more.'

She would not stay. She waddled out of the house and down the front path, and at the front gate met Mr Cook. He had just got out of the car. She gave him a scared little bob of a 'good-day', and scuttled past him and away.

Mr Cook came in wearily; his face was greyish. 'Who was that old dear?' he asked. But he did not really want to know.

His wife said to him, 'Arthur, Judy is going to get your tea – Won't you, love? – while I explain a lot of things. Come and sit down and listen.'

Mrs Cook talked and Mr Cook listened, and gradually his face began to change: something lifted from it, leaving it clear, almost happy, for the first time for many weeks. He was still listening when Judy brought his tea. At the end of Mrs Cook's explanation, Judy added hers: she told her father what – *whom* – she had seen in the garden, when Mrs Baxter had held her hand. Mr Cook began to laugh. 'You saw him, Judy? An old man all in brown with a piece of string tied round his middle – oh, Judy, my girl! When I began really seeing him, only the other day, I was sure I was going off my rocker! I was scared! I thought I was seeing things that no one else could see – things that weren't there at all! And you've seen him too, and he's just old man Baxter!' And Mr Cook laughed so much that he cried, and in the end he put his head down among the tea-things and sobbed and sobbed.

It was going to be all right, after all.

In Mr Baxter's old-fashioned mind, the man of the family was the one to do all the gardening. That was why, in what Judy considered a very unfair way, he had made a dead set at her father. But now all Mr Cook's family rallied to him. Even Mike, when the need was explained, left his bicycle for a while. They all helped in the garden. They dug and weeded and made bonfires of the worst weeds and began to build a compost heap of harmless garden rubbish. They planted seeds if it were not too late in the season, and bought plants when it was. Mr Cook followed the advice of the *Encyclopaedia*, and occasionally had excellent ideas of his own. When Judy asked him where he got them, he looked puzzled at himself and said he did not know. But she could guess.

Every spare moment that was daylight and fine, Mr Cook worked in the garden; and his illness was cured. His appetite came back; he slept like a top; and he would have enjoyed television again except that, in the middle of programmes, he so often fell asleep from healthy exhaustion.

Well over a year later, on a holiday jaunt in Walchester, Judy was passing one of the cinemas. An audience mainly of Senior Citizens was coming out from an afternoon showing of *Deadly Amazon*. Judy felt a touch on her arm, soft yet insistent, like the voice that spoke, Mrs Baxter's: 'My dear, how – how is he?'

'Oh, Mrs Baxter, he's much, much better! Oh, thank you! He's really all right. My mum says my dad's as well as she's ever known him.'

'No, dear, I didn't mean your father. How is *he* – Mr Baxter?'

Judy said, 'We think he's gone. Dad hasn't seen the foggiest wisp of him for months; and Dad says it doesn't *feel* as if he's there any more. You see, Dad's got the garden going wonderfully now. We've had early potatoes and beans and peas – oh, and raspberries – and Dad plans to grow asparagus—'

'Ah,' said Mrs Baxter. 'No wonder Mr Baxter's

gone. Gone off pleased, no doubt. That *is* nice. I don't think you need worry about his coming back. He has enough sense not to. It won't be long before your father can safely give up gardening, if he likes.'

'I'll tell him what you say,' Judy said doubtfully.

But, of course, it was too late. Once a gardener, always a gardener. 'I'll never give up now,' Mr Cook said. 'I'll be a gardener until my dying day.'

'But not after that, Arthur,' said his wife. 'Please.'

Katzenfell

Christobel Mattingley

I never did like the feel of fur. To me it seems eerie somehow. It always made me squeamish to think of the skin of an animal long dead, still transmitting life and warmth.

And when my mother wore her silver fox fur around her neck, I tried not to look at its little feet dangling from her shoulders – feet that had left their footprints on the snow in a far-off land. I tried not to look at its pointed ears which once had heard the wind's songs. And I did not look at all at its eyes or nose, which now were only glass and leather, but which once had seen and smelled sights and scents I would never know.

And I vowed to myself that I would never wear fur – in a coat or a cape, a cap or even a collar. But I did. And a strange thing happened.

It was in Bavaria. And I believe that anything could happen in Bavaria. Beautiful Bavaria, the very heart of Europe. Crowned with mountains whose snow-white peaks exchange secrets with the wind and create mysteries with the clouds. Clothed with deep forests where deer and wild boar live. Studded with villages whose wide-eaved houses and onion-domed churches seem to have come straight out of fairytales.

I had come to study in a famous old Bavarian city and I was living in a tiny room in the garden of the house of an old lady. One night close to Christmas I was coming home late from the library, when I slipped on the icy path. I fell with a force that jarred me right up my spine, and when I pulled myself up carefully and gathered my books which had scattered in the snow, the pain was so great it was all I could do to make my way to my room.

Slowly I peeled off my wet clothes and crawled under the bedcovers. But sleep would not come to blot out my pain and I lay awake in the bitter darkness for hour after hour. Then in the distance I heard a wailing screech which glazed my eyes and froze my fingernails. The sound came closer, closer, until my ears were aching with it. There was a hideous crescendo. Then suddenly it stopped. I lay exhausted, in fearful silence as piercing as my pain.

Sleep came then and when I woke the midwinter sun was probing at the window, making freckles on the wall through the lace curtains. It shone on the icicles hanging from the eave so that they looked like diamond pencils, and I was lying wondering what sort of a story one could write with such a pencil, when a shadow fell on the window.

It was my landlady, a kindly old soul, who nevertheless kept a watchful eye on my comings and goings, as landladies do. She had come to investigate why, by midday, I had not left for the library. When she found me in bed, she tutted and clucked and muttered a mouthful of Bavarian, a dialect I could not understand. Then, after plumping up my pillow, she pulled her shawl over her head and left.

I was dozing, when she came back, carrying an old pewter pot from which steam was curling with smells I could not recognise. When she produced a long-handled spoon, I remembered the saying about supping with the devil, and as she lifted the first spoonful to my mouth, I suddenly wanted to know what it was she was giving me.

As if she read my thoughts she laughed and said in a sing-song voice, 'The breast of a hen, the liver of a pig, the heart of an onion.' She went on chanting a long list of other ingredients as she fed me the broth she had brewed. '*Kräuter und Würze, Kümmel und Kamille, Pilze und Petersilie, Schnittlauch, Knoblauch.*' The German words seemed to weave a spell about my mind as the clear golden broth warmed and soothed my aching body.

She drained the pot to the very last drop of the herb-rich concoction, patted my bedcovers and left, and I slid easily then into a restful sleep.

She woke me when she came the third time. She was carrying a copper kettle from which she poured a deep red liquid into a squat copper mug. I caught my breath on the strong spicy vapours and she smiled and said, '*Zimt und Zucker und Zitrone*, and the wine must be red, always red.' I sipped and the potion ran through me like fire.

She refilled the mug and stood over me while I drank it. Then from under her shawl she produced a soft shapeless bundle.

'*Katzenfell*,' she said, and I wondered if I had heard aright. But now she was unrolling it, holding it out. And there was no doubt.

It was the skin of a cat.

A large cat, a very large cat. Dark grey, almost black with tabby markings of deep burnt orange.

'Fritz,' she said fondly and stroked it as if it were still alive.

I felt sick.

'Warm,' she said, wrapped it round her back and tied it to her with long red strings. Then she took it off, nodded to me and laid it at the foot of my bed.

She meant me to wear it!

My skin prickled. I closed my eyes so that I did not have to look at it.

She chuckled, poured the dregs from the kettle into my mug, put it into my hands and left. I swallowed the last mouthful, which was thick with cinnamon, and fell at once into a curious kind of sleep, where the big feather bedcover seemed to wrap me round like yeasty dough and the pain was slicing through my vertebrae like a knife.

How long I slept I do not know, but it was dark when a movement in the room and a glimmering sort of light woke me. I thought at first it was the old woman again, and called, '*Grüss Gott!*', the traditional Bavarian greeting. But there was no answer and the glimmer disappeared.

I wanted to turn on the light, but I could not move, either for fear or for the pain in my back, I did not know which. I lay in the dark, paralysed, conscious only of the furry shape at my feet, hating it, wishing it would go away. But it did not, and its presence seemed to send little electric shocks up and down my spine.

I shivered. Could there be any truth in the old saying that cats have nine lives? Fritz had obviously been no ordinary cat. But then, and I consoled myself, it must have taken him all of nine lives to grow to such an immense size.

The skin which the old woman had held up was headless. But now there was an occasional golden glint again at the end of the bed. I felt quite certain that I was being watched. Watched by Fritz.

It was not possible, I told myself.

But then I remembered some of the Bavarian folk-tales I had read. And I knew with chill certainty that strange things could happen at midwinter. I broke into an icy sweat and waited.

I found then that my feet, for no reason, seemed to be growing warm, and a vibration was running up my legs. Suddenly, without knowing how or why I did it, I was wrapping the cat fur around me. And in the darkness I was beginning to see the outline of objects in the room, the window, the door. I yawned and stretched, and a ripple of power flowed through me. All my pain had disappeared.

'So, now we are in business,' Fritz said. 'Pleased to meet you.' He gave a chuckle which reverberated through me. 'My old woman is a knowing one. Yes,' he rumbled in satisfaction, 'a very knowing one. She can pick a likely body.'

I got out of bed and moved to the door, walking more easily, more gracefully than I had ever walked before in my life. Fritz was purring, a low hypnotic sound which seemed to take possession of my chest and my ears, my mind and my whole body.

In the distance there was a long screeching wail, like the sound I had heard the night before. I stiffened. Fritz spat. 'The fools,' he hissed. 'Have they forgotten that I was king of the cats for nine years? Do they think they can take over my territory so easily? We'll show them,' he snarled. And I felt my heart beating fast.

As we sprang through the door, Fritz let out a howl which echoed and re-echoed off the nearby buildings, sending icicles shattering to the path. We bounded across the garden and in one leap we were up on a wall abutting the old woman's house. I felt my muscles flex as we crouched for the next longer leap across to a narrow window ledge.

We pressed against the glass and Fritz crooned softly. As a hump in the bed beneath the window moved and murmured in reply, I knew we were looking into the old woman's room.

Then we were off again, up, up, and on to the rooftops. 'I have three scores to settle tonight. And we'll deal with the cats first,' Fritz said. 'We'll put the fear of Fritz back where it belongs.'

We prowled along the ridges of the roofs, peering, prying, leaping from ledge to ledge, listening, looking, skirting clusters of chimney pots gathered together like gossiping old women. We came to a modern block of flats, which seemed rather out of place among the old steep-gabled houses.

We paused. 'Never did like that building,' Fritz said. We looked along the symmetrical rows of staring windows blankly opening on wide balconies, so different from the higgledy-piggledy dormers and attics winking under their tiled eyelids.

Fritz said slowly, 'I have a feeling the trouble is in that box. A pedigreed Pandora in the penthouse maybe. Let's see. It won't take long.'

He walked disdainfully along the outer edge of the balustrade. 'To think that they pulled down perfectly good houses to build this! You couldn't imagine anything more boring. No risk, no challenge. It's an insult to every self-respecting cat. It only encourages them to let their life insurance policies lapse.'

We came to the flat roof which was set out like a garden, with trees in tubs and plants in pots. A table with a furled umbrella and several chairs were folded against a wall.

'Yes,' Fritz repeated, 'there's a chocolate box cat sending out signals from here, and every tom in the district is coming to fight over her. Pussyfeet!' his tone was scathing. 'In my young days it was an adventure to look for a lady on the rooftops. But this! We might as well be walking in the town square.'

Through the glass door of the apartment we glimpsed a simpering fluffy white Persian with a blue satin bow around her neck.

'I told you so,' Fritz said.

While we watched she uttered a low call which was at once answered with strident cries from every quarter. Fritz, with the experience of an old campaigner, ignored the lady, and we took up a strategic position facing all comers, in the shadow of the terrace furniture.

The chorus of cats was coming closer and closer. The white cat was preening herself and smirking as the first suitor came over the balustrade.

He never knew what happened to him. Neither did the next cat, nor the following. Fritz was striking and cuffing, sending cats flying in all directions, and the blanket of night was suddenly rent by shrieks and howls and the crashing of pots and furniture, as the terrified toms tried to escape the silent fury which attacked them.

Fritz caterwauled triumphantly as the last vanquished intruder on his territory tumbled ignominiously out of sight. 'They won't be back in a hurry.'

Then he turned on the vain little Persian who was looking hopefully for the victor from safety behind the glass. 'Get back to your velvet cushion where you belong,' he sneered, 'if you're too scared to get into the act. Calendar cat!'

The white cat gave an outraged mew and a light flashed on in the room. A woman in a velvet dressing gown appeared. She picked up the white cat and exclaimed, 'My poor little precious! Did those nasty alley cats frighten my baby? Hans!' she called.

A sleepy man in pyjamas joined her unwillingly.

'Look at this!' she said to him. 'See what those wretched tom cats have done to our terrace! They've broken all my potplants and they've absolutely terrified my poor little Blossom. She's trembling, aren't you darling?' She cuddled the white cat. 'We'll just have to find another apartment in a better neighbourhood. I've always said this area isn't good enough for Blossom. All these ill-bred alley cats from those old houses. It's like living in the slums.'

I could feel Fritz's fur bristling. He let out such an angry screech that the woman jumped and clutched her husband, dropping the white cat as she did so. It fell in a mewling heap and the man, stepping forward to hold his wife, trod on it. The white cat squealed and sprang up the curtains, knocking over the lampshade and a tall vase of flowers as it went.

Fritz laughed until my belly ached as we made our way past the overturned table and umbrella, pausing on the balustrade while Fritz gloated over the panic and chaos we had created. 'So, we've sent them packing,' he said with satisfaction. 'That was a good warming-up exercise. Now we'll deal with the dog.'

The dog in question was a bad-tempered brute, which did not mind its own business, so Fritz gave me to understand. He did not tell me exactly what the dog had done, but obviously there had been an incident which still rankled with him.

We approached the dog's yard and halted on the wall in the shadow of a large linden tree. Down below there was the chink of a chain and a whimper as the dog twitched in a dream. 'He's remembering me,' Fritz said. 'You see.' He gave a low spitting hiss and the dog jerked awake with a yelp.

I had to admire Fritz's tactics. We stayed out of sight – or could it be that we were invisible? – but Fritz made sure the dog was aware of our presence, taunting him so that the dog was barking in a frenzy of frustration.

A window opened and a man stuck his head out. 'Quiet!' he shouted. 'Lie down!' He slammed the window.

'Quiet! Lie down!' Fritz hissed, and the dog jumped up and began to bark again.

This time the door onto the yard opened and the man came out. 'What's up?' he asked. The dog barked frantically and the man looked round the yard. He flashed a torch into every corner and up along the walls. The dog barked furiously as the torchlight flickered over where we were. But the man saw nothing and turned off the torch.

'You're imagining things,' he told the dog crossly. 'Dreaming. Now go to sleep and let people do the same. Darn dog,' he grumbled as he returned to the house.

Fritz waited a moment to give the man time to go back to bed. Then he called in a low sing-song voice, 'Darn dog is dreaming. Darn dog is dreaming.'

The dog was nearly beside himself. The chain rattled as he pranced and jumped, trying to reach his tormentor, and he barked so desperately that windows began to open in nearby houses, and people began shouting abuse at him. The insults doubled when his owner appeared again, as the neighbours yelled complaints as well as bawling at the dog.

Fritz laughed under his breath as the master began to berate the dog. 'He's got the dog he deserves,' he said. 'A man who doesn't trust his dog can't control him.' He listened for a moment with great satisfaction, then made his final contribution to the hullabaloo he had begun – a nerve-tingling squall that silenced everybody, including the dog.

Fritz chuckled. 'The dog at odds with his master, the master at odds with the dog and the neighbours as well. A neat revenge on an old enemy,' he complimented himself.

'Now for the last account.' Fritz's tone was not pleasant to hear. 'That boy will be longing for daylight after we've called on him.' He said no more, and as we bounded over the roofs, I wondered about the victim of our next visit. He must have teased Fritz at some time. Maybe he had made a habit of it. Whatever it was that he had done, there was no doubt in my mind that he was about to pay heavily for it. But just how heavily I still did not know.

Snow was floating down like feathers, masking paths, filling in footprints, smothering sounds, spreading fresh covers over the existing drifts, which lay in puffs and humps like gigantic eiderdowns over the roofs. And the moonlight threw weird shadows over the white world.

Fritz climbed purposefully towards a high dormer and I knew we were approaching our goal. We jumped onto the ledge and stared in at the window. In a bed below a boy lay sleeping. The boy. I could feel Fritz making him conscious of his presence, needling him through dreams and half remembered happenings. Then suddenly, sharply, the boy awoke, uneasily aware of something strange, something about to happen.

The boy's eyes darted round the room, searching the shadows for unknown shapes, and when his gaze was turned away from the window, Fritz drew his claws down the glass in a sound that set my teeth on edge. The boy looked quickly out, but Fritz was crouching low behind the rim of snow along the window sill. Then as soon as he turned away again, Fritz repeated his action.

The boy sat up and looked out once more. He was shaken, but still in control of himself. Fritz waited. He was very good at waiting. Finally the boy lay down again and pulled the cover over himself.

Fritz waited a little longer. Then he let out the most horrendous shriek I had heard him utter. It seemed to summon every grotesque fear one might have ever had, from all the hidden corners of the mind. The bedcover was trembling and for a long while the boy did not dare to pull it off his head. The moon went behind a cloud and the snow began to fall more heavily. Gradually Fritz's fur was covered with a coat of clinging flakes. But he waited without moving.

Just as the boy began to peer out at last, the moon shone forth with a startling brilliance. Fritz stretched then in one long slow movement and stood up on his hind legs. The reflections of his eyes glowed on the glass. The boy stared in horror and I knew what he was seeing.

'A ghost!' he yelled hoarsely. 'It's a ghost!' He jumped from his bed and we could hear his panic-stricken footsteps thudding down the stairs.

Fritz laughed. A sinister laugh. The boy's terror was the breath of life to him. He said, 'That's taught him not to tease the king of the cats. He'll remember Fritz when every tooth in his gums has rotted and every hair on his scalp has fallen out.'

He stretched his claws. 'I'm hungry. I rather fancy a little snack – a nice plump pigeon, or better still a pair,' he added politely for my benefit.

We headed for the church and walked the dizzy distance along the roof of the nave to the tower. Fritz looked up at the clock. 'Not much time,' he muttered. 'We'll have to hurry.'

We jumped up on to a parapet and began to stalk towards a huddle of pigeons sleeping beneath the clock. We sprang and I was sure that Fritz's claws had found their mark, because I saw a couple of pigeon feathers float by. But then there was a thunderous booming which shook me to the core and all I knew was that snow was sliding and I was falling, falling into darkness.

It was midday when I woke, and although the sun was shining into the room I was cold, because my feather bedcovers had slipped and lay on the floor like a snowdrift from a roof. Only where the cat fur was still wrapped around my back was I warm. I touched the fur gingerly and it seemed to send a shock through me. I stretched and felt my body lithe and completely free of pain.

'Fritz,' I said. I still felt possessed and the memories of the night were vivid.

Could it have happened? Or was it a dream?

I walked to the door. The new snow was dazzling

in the sun, fresh, pure, unmarked. Except for the footprints of a very large cat coming to my door.

I was still staring at them, when the old woman came out of her house. She was carrying a tray. She greeted me with a knowing smile and set the tray on my table. She pulled out a chair for me and patted the fur as I sat down. 'Fritz's favourite,' she said. I thought she meant the milk, which was in a shallow pottery drinking bowl. But she took the lid off a small earthenware cooking pot.

There, floating in a rich brown gravy, was a pair of plump-breasted pigeons.

Time to Laugh

Joan Aiken

When Matt climbed in at the open window of The Croft, it had been raining steadily for three days – August rain, flattening the bronze-green plains of wheat, making dim green jungles of the little woods round Wentby, turning the motorway which cut across the small town's southern tip into a greasy nightmare on which traffic skidded and piled into crunching heaps; all the county police were desperately busy trying to clear up one disaster after another.

If there had been a river at Wentby, Matt might have gone fishing instead, on that Saturday after-noon . . . but the town's full name was Wentby Waterless, the nearest brook was twenty miles away, the rain lay about in scummy pools on the clay, or sank into the lighter soil and vanished. And if the police had not been so manifestly engaged and distracted by the motorway chaos, it might never have occurred to Matt that now would be the perfect time to explore The Croft; after all, by the end of three days' rain, what else was there to do? It had been ten years since the Regent Cinema closed its doors for the last time and went into liquidation.

A Grammar School duffel coat would be too conspicuous and recognisable; Matt wore his black plastic jacket, although it was not particularly rain-proof. But it was at least some protection against the brambles which barred his way.

He had long ago worked out an entry into the Croft grounds, having noticed that they ended in a little triangle of land which bit into the corner of a builder's yard where his father had once briefly worked; Matt had a keen visual memory, never forgot anything he had once observed and, after a single visit two years ago to tell his father that Mum had been taken off to hospital, was able to pick his way without hesitation through cement-mixers, stacks of two-by-two and concrete slabs, to the exact corner, the wattle palings and tangle of elderberry bushes. Kelly never troubled to lock his yard and, in any case, on a Saturday afternoon, no one was about; they were all snug at home, watching telly.

He bored his way through the wet greenery and, as he had reckoned, came to the weed-smothered terrace at the foot of a flight of steps; overgrown shoots of rambler rose half blocked them, but it was just possible to battle upwards, and at the top he was rewarded by a dusky, triangular vista of lawn stretching away on the left towards the house, on the right towards untended vegetable gardens. Amazingly – in the very middle of Wentby – there were rabbits feeding on the lawn, who scattered at his appearance. And between him and the house, two aged, enormous apple trees towered, massive against the murky sky, loaded down with fruit. He had seen them in the aerial photograph of the town, recently exhibited on a school notice-board: that was what had given him the notion of exploring The Croft; you could find out a few things at school if you kept your eyes open and used your wits. He had heard of The Croft before that, of course, but it was nowhere to be seen from any of the town streets: a big house, built in the mid-nineteenth century on an inaccessible plot of land, bought subsequently, after World War Two, by a rich old retired actress and her company-director husband, Lieutenant-Colonel and Mrs Jordan. They were hardly ever seen; never came out, or went anywhere; Matt had a vague idea that one of them – maybe both? – had died. There was a general belief that the house was haunted; also full of treasures; also defended by any number of burglar alarms inside the building, gongs that would start clanging, bells that would ring up at the police station, not to mention man-traps, spring-guns, and savage alsatians outside in the grounds.

However the alsatians did not seem to be in evidence – if they had been, surely the rabbits would not have been feeding so peacefully? So, beginning to disbelieve these tales, Matt picked his way, quietly but with some confidence, over the sodden tussocky grass to the apple trees. The fruit, to his chagrin, was far from ripe. Also they were wretched little apples, codlins possibly, lumpy and mis-shapen, not worth the bother of scrumping. Even the birds appeared to have neglected them; numbers of undersized windfalls lay rotting already on the ground. Angrily, Matt flung a couple against the wall of the house, taking some satisfaction from the squashy thump with which they spattered the stone. The house had not been built of local brick like the rest of Wentby, but from massive chunks of sombre, liver-coloured rock, imported, no doubt at great expense, from farther north. The effect was powerful and ugly; dark as blood, many-gabled and frowning, the building kept guard over its tangled grounds. It seemed deserted; all the windows were lightless, even on such a pouring-wet afternoon; and, prowling round to the front of the house, over a carriage-sweep pocked with grass and weeds, Matt found that the front doorstep had a thin skin of moss over it, as if no foot had trodden there for months. Perhaps the back—? But that was some distance away, and behind a screen of trellis-work and yellow-flecked ornamental laurels. Working on towards it, Matt came to a stop, badly startled at the sight of a half-open window, which, until he reached it, had been concealed from him by a great sagging swatch of untrimmed winter jasmine, whose tiny dark-green leaves were almost black with wet. The coffin-shaped oblong of the open window was black too; Matt stared at it, hypnotised, for almost five minutes, unable to decide whether to go in or not.

Was there somebody inside, there, in the dark? Or had the house been burgled, maybe weeks ago, and the burglar had left the window like that, not troubling to conceal evidence of his entry, because nobody ever came to the place? Or – unnerving thought – was there a burglar inside now, at this minute?

Revolving all these different possibilities, Matt found that he had been moving slowly nearer and nearer to the wall with the window in it; the window was about six feet above ground, but so thickly sleeved around with creeper that climbing in would present no problem at all. The creeper seemed untouched; showed no sign of damage.

Almost without realising that he had come to a decision, Matt found himself digging his toes into the wet mass and pulling himself up – showers of drops flew into his face – until he was able to lean across the window-sill, bracing his elbows against the inner edge of the frame. As might have been expected, the sill inside was swimming with rainwater, the paint starting to crack; evidently the window had been open for hours, maybe days.

Matt stared into the dusky interior, waiting for his eyes to adjust to the dimness. At first, all he could see was vague masses of furniture. Slowly these began to resolve into recognisable forms: tapestried chairs with high backs and bulbous curving legs, side-tables covered in ornaments, a standard lamp with an elaborate pleated shade, dripping tassels, a huge china pot, a flower-patterned carpet, a black shaggy hearthrug, a gold-framed portrait over the mantel. The hearth was fireless, the chair beside it empty, the room sunk in silence. Listening with all his concentration, Matt could hear no sound from anywhere about the house. Encouraged, he swung a knee over the sill, ducked his head and shoulders under the sash, and levered himself in; then, with instinctive caution, he slid down the sash behind him, so that, in the unlikely event of another intruder visiting the garden, the way indoors would not be so enticingly visible.

Matt did not intend to close the window completely, but the sash cord had perished and the heavy frame, once in motion, shot right down before he could stop it; somewhat to his consternation, a little catch clicked across; evidently it was a burglar-proof lock, for he was unable to pull it open again; there was a keyhole in the catch, and he guessed that it could not now be opened again without the key.

Swearing under his breath, Matt turned to survey the room. How would it ever be possible to find the right key in this cluttered, dusky place? It might be in a bowl of odds and ends on the mantelpiece – or in a desk drawer – or hanging on a nail – or in a box – no casual intruder could hope to come across it. Nor – he turned back to inspect the window again – could he hope to smash his way out. The window-panes were too small, the bars too thick. Still, there would be other ways of leaving the house, perhaps he could simply unlock an outside door. He decided that before exploring any farther he had better establish his means of exit, and so took a couple of steps towards a doorway that he could now see on his right. This led through to a large chilly dining-room where a cobwebbed chandelier hung over a massive mahogany dining-table, corralled by eight chairs, and reflecting ghostly grey light from a window beyond. The dining-room window, to Matt's relief, was a case-ment; easy enough to break out of that, he thought, his spirits rising. But perhaps there would be no need, perhaps the burglar-catch was not fastened; and he was about to cross the dining-room and examine it closely when the sound of silvery laughter behind him nearly shocked him out of his wits.

'Aha! Aha! Ha-ha-ha-ha-ha-ha!' trilled the mocking voice, not six feet away. Matt spun round, his heart almost bursting out through his rib-cage. He would have been ready to swear there wasn't a soul in the house. Was it a ghost? Were the stories true, after all?

The room he had first entered still seemed empty, but the laughter had certainly come from that direction, and as he stood in the doorway, staring frantically about him, he heard it again, a long mocking trill, repeated in exactly the same cadence.

'Jesus!' whispered Matt.

And then, as he honestly thought he was on the point of fainting from fright, the explanation was supplied. At exactly the same point from which the laughter had come, a clock began to chime in a thin silvery note obviously intended to match the laughter: *ting, tong, ting, tong.* Four o'clock.

'Jesus,' breathed Matt again. 'How about that? A laughing clock!'

He moved over to inspect the clock. It was a large, elaborate affair, stood on a kind of bureau with brass handles, under a glass dome. The structure of the clock, outworks, whatever you call it, was all gilded and ornamented with gold cherubs who were falling about laughing, throwing their fat little heads back, or doubled up with amusement.

'Very funny,' muttered Matt sourly. 'Almost had me dead of heart-failure, you can laugh!'

Over the clock, he now saw, a big tapestry hung on the wall, which echoed the theme of laughter: girls in frilly tunics this time, and a fat old man sitting on a barrel squashing grapes into his mouth while he hugged a girl to him with the other arm; all of them, too, splitting themselves over some joke, probably a rude one to judge from the old chap's appearance.

Matt wished very much that the clock would strike again, but presumably it would not do that till five o'clock – unless it chimed the quarters; he had better case the rest of the house in the meantime, and reckon to be back in this room by five. Would it be possible to pinch the clock? he wondered. But it looked dauntingly heavy – and probably its mechanism was complicated and delicate, might go wrong if shifted; how could he ever hope to carry it through all those bushes and over the paling fence? And then there would be the problem of explaining its appearance in his father's council flat; he could hardly say that he had found it lying on a rubbish dump. Still he longed to possess it – think what the other guys in the gang would say when they heard it! Maybe he could keep it in Kip Butterworth's house – old Kip, lucky fellow, had a room of his own and such a lot of electronic junk all over it that one clock more or less would never be noticed.

But first he would bring Kip here, at a time just before the clock was due to strike, and let *him* have the fright of his life. . . .

Sniggering to himself at this agreeable thought, Matt turned back towards the dining-room, intending to carry out his original plan of unfastening one of the casement windows, when for the second time he was stopped dead by terror.

A voice behind him said, 'Since you are here, you may as well wind the clock.' And added drily, 'Saturday is its day for winding, so it is just as well you came.'

This time the voice was unmistakably human; trembling like a leaf, Matt was obliged to admit to himself that there was no chance of its being some kind of electronic device – or even a ghost. It was an old woman's voice, harsh, dry, a little shaky, but resonant; only, where the devil *was* she?

Then he saw that what he had taken for a wall

beyond the fireplace was, in fact, one of those dangling bamboo curtains, and beyond it – another bad moment for Matt – was this motionless figure sitting on a chair, watching him; had been watching him – must have – all the time, ever since he had climbed in, for the part of the room beyond the curtain was just a kind of alcove, a big bay window really, leading nowhere. She must have been there all the time. . . .

'Go on,' she repeated, watching Matt steadily from out of her black triangle of eyes, 'wind the clock.'

He found his voice and said hoarsely, 'Where's the key, then?'

'In the round bowl on the left side.'

His heart leapt; perhaps the window key would be there too. But it was not; there was only one key: a long heavy brass shaft with a cross-piece at one end and a lot of fluting at the other.

'Lift the dome off; carefully,' she said. 'You'll find two keyholes in the face. Wind them both. One's for the clock, the other for the chime.'

And, as he lifted off the dome and began winding, she added thoughtfully, 'My husband made that clock for me, on my thirtieth birthday. It's a recording of my own voice – the laugh. Uncommon, isn't it? He was an electrical engineer, you see. Clocks were his hobby. All kinds of unusual ones he invented – there was a Shakespearean clock, and a barking dog, and one that sang hymns – my voice again. I had a beautiful singing voice in those days – and my laugh was famous of course. 'Miss Langdale's crystalline laugh,' the critics used to call it. . . . My husband was making a skull clock just before he died. There's the skull.'

There it was, to be sure, a real skull, perched on top of the big china jar to the right of the clock.

Vaguely now, Matt remembered reports of her husband's death; wasn't there something a bit odd about it? Found dead of heart-failure in the underpass below the motorway, at least a mile from his house; what had he been *doing* there, in the middle of the night? Why walk through the underpass, which was not intended for pedestrians anyway?

'He was going to get some cigarettes when he died,' she went on, and Matt jumped; had she read his thoughts? How could she know so uncannily what was going through his head?

'I've given up smoking since then,' she went on. 'Had to, really . . . They won't deliver, you see. Some things you can get delivered, so I make do with what I can get. I don't like people coming to the house too often, because they scare the birds. I'm a great bird person, you know—'

Unless she has a servant, then, she's alone in the house, Matt thought, as she talked on, in her sharp, dry old voice. He began to feel less terrified – perhaps he could just scare her into letting him leave. Perhaps, anyway, she was mad?

'Are you going to phone the police?' he asked boldly. 'I wasn't going to pinch anything, you know – just came in to have a look-see.'

'My dear boy, I don't care *why* you came in. As you *are* here, you might as well make yourself useful. Go into the dining-room, will you, and bring back some of those bottles.'

The rain had abated, just a little, and the dining-room was some degrees lighter when he walked through into it. All along the window wall Matt was amazed to see wooden wine-racks filled with bottles and half-bottles of champagne. There must be hundreds. There were also, in two large log baskets beside the empty grate, dozens of empties. An armchair was drawn close to an electric bar-fire, not switched on; a half-empty glass and bottle stood on a silver tray on the floor beside the armchair.

'Bring a glass, too,' Mrs Jordan called.

And, when he returned with the glass, the tray, and several bottles under his arm, she said, 'Now, open one of them. You know how to, I hope?'

He had seen it done on TV; he managed it without difficulty.

'Ought to be chilled, of course,' she remarked, receiving the glass from him. One of her hands lay limply on the arm of the chair – she hitched it up from time to time with the other hand when it slipped off; and, now that he came near to her for the first time, he noticed that she smelt very bad; a strange, fetid smell of dry unwashed old age and something worse. He began to suspect that perhaps she was *unable* to move from her chair. Curiously enough, instead of this making him fear her less, it made him fear her more. Although she seemed a skinny, frail old creature, her face was quite full in shape, pale and puffy like underdone pastry. It must have been handsome once – long ago – like a wicked fairy pretending to be a princess in a kid's book illustration; now she just looked spiteful and secretive, grinning down at her glass of bubbly. Her hair, the colour of old dry straw, was done very fancy, piled up on top of her head. Perhaps it was a wig?

'Get a glass for yourself, if you want,' she said. 'There are some more in the dining-room cupboard.'

He half thought of zipping out through the dining-room window while he was in there; but still, he was curious to try the fizz, and there didn't seem to be any hurry, really. It was pretty plain the old girl wasn't going anywhere, couldn't be any actual danger to him, although she did rather give him the gooeys. Also he did want to hear that chime again.

As he was taking a glass out from the shimmering ranks in the cupboard, a marvellous thought struck him: Why not bring all the gang here for a banquet? Look at those hundreds and hundreds of bottles of champagne – what a waste, not to make use of them! Plainly *she* was never going to get through them all – not in the state she was in. Maybe he could find some tinned stuff in the house too – but anyway, they could bring their own grub with them, hamburgers and crisps or stuff from the Chinese Takeaway – if the old girl was actually paralysed in her chair, she couldn't stop them. . . . In fact it would add to the fun, the excitement, having her there. They could fetch her in from the next room, drink her health in her own bubbly; better not leave it too long, though, didn't seem likely she could last more than a few more days.

Candles, he thought, we'd have to bring candles; and at that point her voice cut into his thoughts, calling, 'Bring the two candles that are standing on the cupboard.'

He started violently – but it was only a coincidence, after all – picked up the candles in their tall cut-glass sticks and carried them next door with a tumbler for himself.

'Matches on the mantel,' she said.

The matches were in a fancy enamel box. He lit the candles and put them on the little table beside her. Now he could see more plainly that there was something extremely queer about her: her face was all drawn down one side, and half of it didn't seem to work very well.

'Electricity cut off,' she said. 'Forgot to pay the bill.'

Her left hand was still working all right, and she had swallowed down two glasses in quick succession, refilling them herself each time from the opened bottle at her elbow. 'Fill your glass,' she said, slurring the words a little.

He was very thirsty – kippers and baked beans they always had for Saturday midday dinner, and the fright had dried up his mouth too – like Mrs Jordan he tossed down two glasses one after the other. They fizzed a bit – otherwise they didn't have much taste.

'Better open another bottle,' she said. 'One doesn't go anywhere between two. Fetch in a few more while you're up, why don't you?'

'She's planning,' he thought to himself; 'knows she can't move from that chair, so she wants to be stocked up for when I've gone.' He wondered if in fact there was a phone in the house? Ought he to ring for a doctor, the police, an ambulance? But then he would have to account for his presence. And he and the gang would never get to have their banquet; the windows would be boarded up for sure, she'd be carted off to the Royal West Midland geriatric ward, like Auntie Glad after her stroke.

'There isn't a phone in the house,' said Mrs Jordan calmly. 'I had it taken out after Jock died; the bell disturbed the birds. That's right, put them all down by my chair, where I can reach them.'

He opened another bottle, filled both their glasses, then went back to the other room for a third load.

'You like the clock, don't you,' she said, as he paused by it, coming back.

'Yeah. It's uncommon.'

'It'll strike the quarter in a minute,' she said, and soon it did – a low, rather malicious chuckle, just a brief spurt of sound. It made the hair prickle on the back of Matt's neck, but he thought again, Just wait till the rest of the gang hear that! A really spooky sound.

'I don't want you making off with it, though,' she said. 'No, no, that would never do. I like to sit here and listen to it.'

'I wasn't going to take it!'

'No, well, that's as maybe.' Her triangular black eyes in their hollows laughed down at him – he was squatting on the carpet near her chair, easing out a particularly obstinate cork. 'I'm not taking any chances. Eight days – that clock goes for eight days. Did you wind up the chime too?'

'Yeah, yeah,' he said impatiently, tipping more straw-coloured fizz into their glasses. Through the pale liquid in the tumbler he still seemed to see her eyes staring at him shrewdly.

'Put your glass down a moment,' she said. 'On the floor – that will do. Now, just look here a moment.' She was holding up her skinny forefinger. Past it he could see those two dark triangles. 'That's right. Now – watch my finger – you are very tired, aren't you? You are going to lie down on the floor and go to sleep. You will sleep – very comfortably – for ten minutes. When you wake, you will walk over to that door and lock it. The key is in the lock. Then you will take out the key and push it under the door with one of the knitting-needles that are lying on the small table by the door. Ahhh! You are so sleepy.' She

yawned, deeply. Matt was yawning too. His head
flopped sideways on to the carpet and he lay motionless, deep asleep.

While he slept it was very quiet in the room. The
house was too secluded in its own grounds among the
builder's yards for any sound from the town to reach
it; only faintly from far away came the throb of the
motorway. Mrs Jordan sat impassively listening to it.
She did not sleep; she had done enough sleeping and
soon would sleep even deeper. She sat listening, and
thinking about her husband; sometimes the lopsided
smile crooked down one corner of her mouth.

After ten minutes the sleeping boy woke up.
Drowsily he staggered to his feet, walked over to the
door, locked it, removed the key, and, with a long
wooden knitting-needle, thrust it far underneath and
out across the polished dining-room floor.

Returning to the old lady he stared at her in a
vaguely bewildered manner, rubbing one hand up
over his forehead.

'My head aches,' he said in a grumbling tone.

'You need a drink. Open another bottle,' she said.
'Listen: the clock is going to strike the half-hour.'

On the other side of the room the clock gave its
silvery chuckle.

Time, and Time Again

Judith Butler

Polly knew something was going on. Ever since the party had entered the Long Gallery, she had sensed that someone was trying to get through to her. It was no good saying anything: nobody understood.

Even as a very little girl, Polly had a special sensitivity to the atmosphere of buildings. It first came out when she was about six. A great aunt had recently died, leaving two unmarried sisters. Polly was told nothing about it, and picked up no inkling from conversation. Her mother simply said they were going to visit two old aunts of Daddy's and she must behave quietly because they were so old and used to an undisturbed life.

When they got there, Polly was sent to play in the garden, but happened to come indoors just as her mother was being shown upstairs to the late relative's bedroom, to choose some small memento. Polly trotted upstairs after her, and as the bedroom door was opened, bounced ahead into the room.

At once the consciousness of recent death – the

failing senses, the last desperate but feeble struggle, the swift darkness closing in – rushed about her head, and she screamed out:

'Mummy! Mummy! Don't come in! Someone's been dead in here!'

After that she often found that she could tell what sort of lives had been lived in a house by just standing still and listening – or smelling – or feeling. She was not sure what senses she used.

Many people do not like to think about things they do not understand, and Polly's mother managed to dismiss the whole thing. If Polly thought about it at all, she supposed it was nothing special and that everyone must feel things the way she did. Until one day when she was about fourteen, and the history class was taken to visit an old church. Trailing slowly round with a group can be tiring to the feet, and Polly sat down, with her friend Janice, in one of the pews. All at once Polly turned pale, looked as if she were about to cry, and saying, 'Oh, no! How dreadful – I can't bear it!' she hastily got up and moved to another row.

'Whatever's the matter?' whispered Janice. 'Feel faint or something?'

'What? Oh, no, I'm all right over here. It was just that place. There was this woman, you see, and her little boy was very ill and she felt sure he was going to die, and she worried so much and prayed so hard – oh, it was dreadful, I never thought anyone could feel so absolutely awful, as if the bottom was falling out of their life.'

'What woman?'

'Oh, I don't know who. Just somebody who came here pretty regularly. Quite a long time ago, but the feeling's still there. Like when you've stood something too hot on a table and the mark of it stays there for ages afterwards. Don't you ever get sort of messages about places?'

'No – I – do – *not*,' said Janice, and gave her friend a very funny look.

Polly kept any future 'messages' to herself.

Now Polly was older, with only half a term of school life to come, and the days were almost too full. Therefore, it was a surprise to her parents and almost to herself when she suddenly asked if she might join them on the coach party. It was a splendid afternoon in late May, and a group of people, mostly middle-aged and elderly, planned a drive through the countryside to one of the 'stately homes' recently re-opened for the summer season, followed by a meal at a riverside inn. There were one or two vacant seats on the coach, so Polly had been able to go along, and despite being the only really young person present had genuinely enjoyed the outing so far. Now, in the Long Gallery, she was enjoying it still, though beginning to be troubled by something as yet only fragmentarily understood.

In such a huge house, home for centuries of a large and famous family, the atmosphere was bound to be tumultuous with evidence of past lives. Polly felt that confusion and probably headache would result if she stopped deliberately to pick up whatever 'messages' were emanating from the panelled walls, the ornate ceilings, the furniture's polished wood or faded upholstery. She had therefore concentrated on listening to the guide, a jolly woman who, despite obviously knowing the history of the place off by heart and able to repeat it word for word to each succeeding party of visitors, nevertheless managed to convey to them some of her own affection for the house.

They had toured the ground floor and the East Wing and began the ascent of the enormous sweeping staircase lined with family portraits, beginning at the bottom with the most recent: the present Viscount in his robes as Chancellor of the local and recently-founded university. Here was the old Earl in uniform, painted just before he went to the Front in 1915 . . . a rosy young Marchioness in expanses of white muslin, by Sargent . . . an earlier, Scottish one, painted before her marriage by Raeburn. Now a line of still earlier pictures stretched ahead down the Long Gallery, with dusty gold fans of afternoon sunlight slanting through the tall windows which alternated with paintings . . . the fourth Earl, with cocked hat and gun and favourite spaniel, by Gainsborough, portrayed proudly in his newly-planted park, his newly-completed house in the background. This gallery, explained the guide, was one of the oldest parts of the original building: the classical portico and wings had been added as the family prospered. . . .

It was at this point that Polly fell a little behind the group, so that she could hear the voice of the guide less clearly and the other voice — or whatever it was — better. It was rather, she reflected, like persistent interference on radio, but intermittent, as if unused to the wavelength of the twentieth century.

'What is so odd,' she thought, 'is that it seems to be wanting to speak to *me*, in particular.'

If only she could make out the words.

'. . . lady!' she heard at last. Then, more clearly, 'Young lady . . . young Madam . . . whoever you may be. . . .'

'I'm Polly — Pauline — Sandell,' she answered inside her head, but evidently whatever it was could

not read thoughts, for the voice took no notice, but
went on with more insistence:

'Can you hear nothing, see nothing? Oh, and I
have essayed time and time again! Tell me, if you can
hear – tell me who you are!'

This time Polly raised the flap of her handbag, as if
searching for a handkerchief, bent her head, and
behind this cover whispered her name again, adding,
'Who are you?'

The reply came from so close to her ear that Polly
jumped.

'Hearken to the guide. Then come away to the
window.'

Puzzled but not frightened, Polly caught up with
the group. They had paused before the portrait of a
girl, pale and thin, her dark hair in loose ringlets. She
wore a pale blue silk dress with wide sleeves, the low
neck outlined in gold braid and filled in with folds of
lace. This was fastened to the centre of the dress by
an enormous gold brooch. It had a bluish stone
surrounded by pearls in the centre, with five pearl
drops below.

'. . . and she was named Marina,' the guide was
saying, 'because she was actually born at sea. Her
parents both belonged to families which went into
exile with Charles II, and they married in France. It
was Sir John's loyalty to King Charles which got him
an earldom at the Restoration. Sir John and his
young wife came back with other members of the
court, and their third child, a daughter, was born
before they reached the English coast.'

'She doesn't look very strong,' remarked one of the
visitors.

'You're quite right, she wasn't. She died at seven-
teen, shortly before she was due to be married. This

portrait was painted to celebrate the betrothal. The brooch she is wearing was an engagement present from the man she was to have married. If you look closely you will see that the gold setting is in the form of a mermaid and merman surrounding an aquamarine set with pearls – a charming tribute to her name, Marina. It was, of course, highly valuable and would no doubt have become a notable heirloom, but the mysterious thing is that after Marina's death the brooch could not be found and has never been seen since. Now here we come to . . .'

Polly was startled to feel a light touch on her hand. She wandered across to the nearest window, as if she wanted to look at the view over the park. Something followed her, and touched her hand again.

'Marina?' she whispered.

'Can you see me?'

'No,' said Polly; but then she added, 'Well, sort of. Against that curtain. If I look hard, I can't see you at all, but if I look away and then quickly back again, I do see you for a moment before the curtain starts coming through again. You're very like your portrait. But why have you come through to me? What do you want?'

'You can release me and let me rest,' said the gentle voice, 'and not me only. You can find another spirit, restless and distressed as mine, and give him, too, peace – as I long to do, but cannot without aid from the living. Stay when the rest have gone, and come to me here, I beg you. . . .'

Polly blinked, and saw only a faded red velvet curtain, and the afternoon sunlight over the park.

'Come along, love,' called her mother. The visitors were passing the place where she stood.

'We have to go back by the same stairs,' the guide

was explaining. 'There *is* a way down at this end, but it leads to the family's rooms. They don't keep much of the house for their own use, and naturally we're careful to respect their privacy.'

'It must be a terrible responsibility, a place like this,' remarked Polly's mother. 'You can't just sell it. And what the upkeep must be! I mean, they must need the money badly to put up with droves of strangers tramping round all the time. And did you see that room marked *Private* that we passed downstairs? The door was a bit open, and you could see – well, I'd be ashamed if it was mine. Carpet worn into holes, stuffing coming out of the chairs – I mean, what's the use of putting all these lovely antiques on show if you can't have a bit of comfort yourself. . . .'

She chattered on as the party went over the rest of the house. Polly paid little attention. How would it be possible to stay behind? And yet she must.

'And finally, ladies and gentlemen, if you would care to follow me back to the hall where we began the tour, you will find postcards and leaflets on sale at the desk.'

'And a box for tips, no doubt,' murmured Polly's mother. 'My feet are killing me – I think I'll just go back to the coach and wait for the rest of you there. Dad can put something in the box.'

'I'll do it,' offered Polly. 'You don't want any cards, Dad, do you? You go with Mum, and I'll go back with the others and join you later.'

Another party was already gathering in the hall, this time with an elderly man as guide. Polly looked quickly round. There! By the front door stood an old-fashioned porter's chair, its back very tall and curved into a deep leather hood designed to keep draughts off the servant on door duty. It no longer stood in its proper place, but had been turned to the wall, out of the way of the crowds passing. Polly slipped over to it, and curled up on its seat. She was invisible, secret and safe.

In a few minutes the hall grew quiet. Her own party had gone to find its coach, and the new people had been taken to the East Wing. Polly peeped round the hood. A middle-aged lady was sitting at the desk which held entrance tickets and postcards. She was knitting. A black labrador dog lay dozing at her feet. Suddenly, the dog jumped up, barking wildly. It rushed to the foot of the staircase and pranced about, growling between barks, the hairs on its neck standing up like a ruff. Every now and then it made as if to mount the stairs, but fell back, the growls dying off into whimpers of fright. The lady had jumped to her feet, too, crying:

'Whatever's wrong with you, Ben? Stop it! Stop that noise this moment! Well, if you won't behave, you bad dog, you'll have to go. You've got to learn to be nice to visitors. Come along!' Seizing his collar, she dragged him away.

Polly could see what Ben was barking at. At the top of the staircase stood Marina, much clearer now. Polly darted from her hiding place and up the stairs. Marina had gone ahead of her, and was waiting near her portrait.

'We haven't much time.'

'Time means nothing to me now,' said the ghost. 'I no longer recall how it feels to have time, or have no time. I can only tell that it is pain – great pain – to be dragged back to the edge of time.'

'But,' asked Polly, her curiosity getting the better of her tact, 'why aren't you in heaven? Or isn't heaven true, after all?'

Marina sighed.

'How can I make you understand? It is as if I have woken from dreaming, but no longer recall the dream. I know that *it* – heaven, eternity, what you will – is where I belong, but when called back into time by earthly duties unfulfilled, I have no memory of any heavenly state, only of my brief mortal life.'

'I'm sorry,' was all Polly could think of to say. 'You were so young.'

'I was ever a sickly child. After the fevers, the coughs, the agues and swoonings which plagued me, I was glad to die.'

'But weren't you engaged to be married?'

'That was no great felicity. Had I married, I could not have borne children and lived, nor was it likely any child of mine could have survived. But here's the heart of the matter. My father betrothed me to a man twice my age; he thought to do me good by marrying me to one who had great estates, riches in plenty and, to do him justice, a kind heart. My brothers supported the match for they thought that by this connection they might gain riches and preferment. As it was, because it was not thought that I could produce a child, it was written into the marriage agreement that certain possessions should revert to my family.'

'And didn't you like this man?'

'He was well enough, in his way. But I had met someone else, a young man of barely twenty. We fell fathoms deep in love. His family had lost lands and fortune in the late wars between Crown and Parliament. So he had little to recommend him to my father and brothers, and finding they could not part us, my brothers set out to trap him.'

'What, beat him up or murder him or something?'

'At first they were more subtle. They found the

lewdest girls in all the neighbourhood and bribed the sluts to ensnare him, but he would have none of them. They paid fellows to drink with him and then, when he had well drunk and was not himself, provoke a brawl, but he held out manfully. Then one day one of these hired scoundrels called – called my honour in question, and my – my dearest love was in honour bound to fight him. He killed the man, and knew that he must fly the country. He came to bid my farewell, secretly. He had but little money and I gave him my brooch, the richest object I had ever possessed. It was the gift of my future husband, and should have formed part of the wealth of my family. Ill-omened gift! Seeing I no longer wore my brooch, my brothers guessed something of the matter, and the very night he was to have fled waylaid him.'

'Excuse my interrupting,' said Polly, 'but did he live close by, then?'

'At Sapden Hall.'

'Wait!' whispered Polly. 'People are coming. It must be that other party of visitors. They can't find me here, talking to you, talking to nothing!'

'I have almost done,' said the ghost. 'The rest is soon told. They slew him. There was no proof, no body, but all our household guessed at the deed, and as I lay dying, my eldest brother confessed it to me, and told me that my lover had made them promise to restore the brooch to me, but that he died e'er he could tell them where it lay. They sought the jewel but could find no trace. And so we walk: dead, but not at peace. You, Polly Sandell, who can bridge the stream of time and hear my tale – find it, and give us rest!'

'And here, ladies and gentlemen, we enter the Long Gallery. . . .'

Marina was gone, and Polly looked wildly round

for a way out. Already the guide was looking at her suspiciously as he advanced. Polly remembered what the lady had said about another stairway at this end. She turned and fled.

She barged through a door marked 'Private' and was unprepared for the flight of steps immediately on the other side. She hurtled down, clutching vainly at the banister. Finally she managed to grasp it, but was too off-balance to run down the rest of the flight properly. Sliding far too fast for comfort, she finally overbalanced again and landed in a bunch at the bottom, butting her head hard against a pair of knees in blue jeans. She put up a hand to save herself, and grabbed a fistful of yellow sweater.

'Hey-up, steady does it!' said their owner. He was a boy not much older than she was. He had been walking along the passage at the foot of the stairs, carrying a bundle of rags, but Polly didn't stop to look at him.

'Sorry!' she gasped. 'Whereza – way – out?'

'Here we are,' said the boy, leading the way. 'Hang on, though: are you sure you're okay? Want to sit down a minute?'

'No, no – I'll miss the coach – I'm all right – thanks a lot. . . .'

They had come out into a yard behind the stable block. In the middle of it stood a small red car. Beyond an archway Polly could see a wide stretch of cobblestones which she recognised as the main court-yard leading off the front drive, the way visitors came in. She dashed across, and reached the archway just in time to see the back of the coach vanishing towards the gates.

Polly leaned against the wall and closed her eyes. She felt weak.

'Not to worry,' said the boy, who had come over and was standing beside her. 'We can soon catch that lot up. Where are they heading for, anyway?'

Polly opened her eyes and looked at him. He had a long, pale, good-humoured face and a lot of coarse, wavy hair between red and chestnut, which stood out like a halo of copper wire.

'They're going to the Swan, just outside Langwell,' she told him. 'There's a meal laid on. There'll be trouble if I don't turn up, because they'll have ordered for me and they'll have to pay for it just the same. Is there a bus or anything?'

The boy grinned, and waved his bundle of rags at the red mini.

'Better than a bus. I was just going to give her a polish up, but that can wait. Hop in.'

Polly hesitated.

'Go on, it's all right. You can trust me. I live here. Go and ask my mother, if you like – she's in the front hall, sitting at the receipt of custom. My name's Giles Hornabrook.'

Of course. This was Hornabrook House. But to be sure, Polly said, 'Does that make you, er, a son of the Viscount that the guide talked about?'

'That's right. Did she tell you about the name? Probably someone obscure who lived at the Corner of the Brook, and it gradually got corrupted because nobody bothered about spelling, and very wise, too. Look: are you coming?'

Polly decided to trust Giles, if only because she dared not go back into the hall: she had an idea she would find Giles's mother being anxiously questioned by the old guide man as to whether a young lady had gone running past. . . .

On the way to Langwell, she said casually, 'The

guide didn't say anything about a family ghost, or anything like that. You'd think in such a big old place there might be a legend or two.'

Giles grinned.

'I wouldn't know. I mean, we're an awfully prosaic lot. The place could be stuffed with phantoms and we'd never notice. Hey – wait a minute though: you bolted down that staircase like a scared rabbit. Did you think there was a – but what were you doing there anyway? That's our bit of the house, and your party had already gone back to the coach.'

'If I was trespassing, I'm sorry,' said Polly stiffly. 'I wasn't being nosy, if that's what you mean. And it wasn't *her* I was running away from, either. She wasn't at all frightening, even if she was a gho—'

'Oh God,' said Giles. 'The Long Gallery again.'

'So there *is* something, then?'

'Well, like I said, none of us notices anything like that. But we've had one or two visitors nearly having hysterics up there. One woman swore blind that something sighed and touched her hand.'

'That's right,' said Polly. 'Your dog Ben saw it, too. Your mother didn't know what he was on about, and took him away.'

'It's the same with all dogs,' Giles agreed. 'Won't go near the Long Gallery if they can help, and if you do take them up there for any reason, they tremble all over. I haven't a clue who or what it's supposed to be, though.'

'Well I know,' said Polly. And she told him.

Giles was silent for a few moments. Then he said:

'Look, I can't *not* believe you. I do believe you. But you could have read it beforehand and been sort of expecting it, subconsciously. I mean, that story of the murder is a sort of family legend. The guides don't include it in their spiel, because it's not authenticated, but it was mentioned in a family history that some old boy wrote, round about 1910, I think. So you might just about have seen that and had it at the back of your mind, couldn't you?'

'I knew nothing whatever about it; I'd scarcely even heard of your family before tonight, and anyway, I've always been able to sort of feel what's been going on in places.' She told him about the great aunt's bedroom, and about the church pew with its burden of sorrow.

'Well, it's very peculiar,' agreed Giles, who didn't seem disposed to take the matter too seriously. 'Did you say this bloke came from Sapden Hall, and left this brooch lying around there somewhere? I must have a look sometime, if the bulldozers didn't bury it for good, putting the new blocks up.'

'What is Sapden Hall, then?'

'Don't you know? The university of the South Midlands?'

'Oh, that place. But I thought it was new.'

'So it is, as a University, but they only got it started because the Sapden Estate was left to them – something to do with death duties. The original old house, Sapden Hall, is still there. It's all been turned into common rooms and restaurants and things; I use it a lot.'

'Of course. Your father's Chancellor.'

'Yes, and I'm a second-year student. Civil Engineering. Any objections?'

'I thought people like you went to Oxford or Cambridge or else nowhere at all.'

'What d'you mean, people like me? I couldn't have got into Cambridge on my A-levels – two D's and an E. I was lucky to get in anywhere, and get a grant and all. My lot couldn't have managed it otherwise. D'you realise that lumping great house just eats all my family's money, the bit that doesn't go in taxes? Anyway, I've got in touch with one of these big contractors, building motorways, new towns, that sort of thing, so *if* I get a decent degree, because they're a super-efficient outfit, there's a job for me there.'

'And the best of British luck,' said Polly. 'I'm going to a tech to do a catering course. But listen, about Marina: could you really do anything?'

'I'll think about it, and let you know. I'd be chuffed to get that brooch back. I mean, it would be like having it restored to Marina, wouldn't it?'

It was a month before Giles telephoned. In the meantime Polly had tried to stop herself from building a delightful fantasy. They found the brooch, of course, and Giles was spellbound by her sensitivity and intuition, and deeply impressed by her unselfishness in giving time and effort to a cause from which she, personally could never benefit. So what better destiny for the brooch than for the restored heirloom to become the gift of the heir to his fiancée. . . .'

'Stupid twit,' said Polly to herself, crossly.

Giles said over the phone, 'For the first time ever, and I trust the last, I've used the fact of my father's being the super-boss to my own advantage. I got him to encourage the Civil Engineering Department to buy a most useful gadget, a metal-detector. It looks a bit like a flat vacuum cleaner, and when you pass it over any hidden metal, it bleeps, so you know where to start looking. And I've also got permission to stay up after the end of term. Work, I said. So it is, of a kind.'

'I'm with you,' said Polly. 'You're going to go over

the house with this thing, and see if you can locate the brooch – right?'

'We've done that already. Sarah stayed up too, and we've spent a couple of days on it. Turned up no end of nails and rubbish, but no proper clue.'

'Who's Sarah?'

'My girl-friend. She's the same year as me, but on the Arts side. She's got really keen on this thing, now I've told her all about it, and we agreed that we ought to ask you to come over and help us, if you wouldn't mind.'

'Well that *is* nice,' said Polly, and hoped she sounded less sarcastic than she felt.

Giles and Sarah (who was dumpy and dark and rather fierce) fetched her in the red mini. Giles had made a plan of Sapden Hall. He kept a copy for himself and Sarah, and gave one to Polly.

'It's been so altered, while it was being modernised,' he said, 'there may well be bits we missed the first time round. So we're going to have another go, and we thought that perhaps you'd like to have a wander round, see if your peculiar radar or whatever it is picks up any hints. Okay?'

Polly was irritated by this 'we', and still more irritated when she realised that she had no reason to be. After all, she had only met Giles once before, and they really hadn't much in common. Sarah was scowling, as if daring her to disagree with anything Giles proposed.

'What makes you think it has to be in the house? Couldn't it have been hidden outside somewhere?'

'It just could have,' Giles agreed, 'but we don't think it's likely. We talked it over – didn't we, Sarah? – and we decided to make dead sure about the house first, before we start asking for permission to dig up the park.'

'After all,' put in Sarah, 'he was about to start on a journey and intended taking the brooch with him, so it wouldn't have been far away. It's just that for some reason the murderers didn't guess where, and it must be somewhere that hasn't been disturbed since.'

Polly thought childishly, *Marina told all this to me, not you, Miss Clever*, and realised she was plain jealous. She was furious with herself. Giles produced the machine and despite having to lug it about managed to leave an arm free for entwining round Sarah. They trailed off to start their search. By now thoroughly disgruntled, Polly took her plan to the top of the house, and began working methodically downwards.

It was a bad day for 'messages'. Her own feelings were too active, her personal affairs occupied too much of her mind. The house yielded nothing. After an hour or so of wandering about on her own she felt tired, foot-sore, lonely and depressed. Attracted by the sunlight, she dawdled out into the quiet grounds, and walked slowly round the gravel paths. She crossed what was once a terrace, now levelled as a car park, and at the back of the house, through a gateway in a wall, she found a stable yard not unlike the one at Hornabrook House. The stables still existed but, as Polly found when she began to explore, they now held motor-mowers, barrows, tools and the like. There was nobody about. Polly felt utterly bored, and was on the point of going back to find the others, when she was conscious of being strangely ill at ease.

She leaned against the nearest door post as the feeling grew stronger. It was a blazing June day, and she was standing on the sunny side of the yard, but found she was shivering. All at once she was vividly reminded of that day long ago in the old lady's bedroom: she had the same illusion of being caught up with someone who was vainly fighting off an overwhelming onslaught on the senses. And even as she whispered to herself, '*Death*', there came a kind of whispering echo just behind her.

'Sweet Marina, though I fall—' it gasped and then ended in a kind of thick choking gurgle, a terrible sound.

Now that she had picked it up, Polly heard the voice over and over again:

'Sweet Marina, though I fall . . . Sweet Marina, though I fall . . . Sweet Marina. . . .'

It was more than she could stand. She ran for the house, calling out for Giles.

Giles and Sarah came running in glad expectation of a find, but their smiles faded at the sight of Polly's white face. She told them what she had heard, and led the way. The other two, standing amid the brooms and boxes, the coils of hose and cans of paraffin, heard nothing, felt nothing, and stared at Polly who was turning almost yellow. All at once, she cried out:

'Oh, I wish he didn't have to keep doing that – it makes me feel sick!'

'What does?'

'That noise. He gets so far, and then he sort of gags, and chokes. Ugh, it's horrible. Time and time again, over and over, he tries to get the words out but the pain suddenly hits him.'

'Like a crack in a record?' asked Sarah.

'Exactly that. As if all the things he felt at that instant – the shock of being attacked, and the pain of the wound, and the realisation that he was dying there and then, and the frustration at not being able

to get any message to Marina – as if all this added up
to such an intensity of feeling that it sort of grooved
itself into the spot where it all took place. I'm going
outside where I can't hear it.'

'Poor kid,' said Sarah. 'After that, I think I'm glad
I wasn't born with that sort of gift. What are we going
to do, Giles? See if your contraption indicates anything?'

'May as well. Mind you, although this may be – I
believe it must be – where the poor chap finished up,
it doesn't actually tell us any more about where the
brooch is. Still, it's a clue, a connection. Tell you
what: never mind fetching the bleeper – let's just dig
up a few of these old bricks out of the floor, and see if
there's any sort of a further clue underneath.'

In one of the other ex-stables they found spades
and trowels, and an iron bar for levering up the
ancient floor stones. It was extremely hard work, but
once the top layer was off the ground became softer
and the digging easier.

'Polly,' asked Giles suddenly. 'That voice – can
you still hear it?'

Polly paused a moment before answering.

'Yes, but it's different, a bit. It's gone sort of
quivery, as if the sounds were being disturbed.'

'Hey, look!' cried Sarah, and pulled out of the hole
a piece of metal with earth clinging to it. Even when
wiped it was almost too eaten with corrosion to be
recognisable, but they could see that it had once been
a sword, and that it was still in its scabbard, welded
to it with rust.

'If that's his,' remarked Giles, 'it looks as if he
didn't have time to draw it – he must have been taken
completely by surprise.'

'And to think I was about to suggest we gave up,'

said Sarah. 'I'm so hot and exhausted. But we simply must go on now we've found that. It certainly ties up with what you said, Polly, about extreme shock, I mean if he didn't even get a chance to fight but simply got clobbered.'

'There's a tap in the yard,' remarked Giles. 'I suppose what they run these hoses off. Let's hope it's drinkable – I could work a lot better after a drink of water.'

They all worked better, and after a few more minutes digging – 'Hold it!' called Giles, and bent down. This time it was the black and mouldered relic of a leather strap or belt, with part of a metal buckle. Polly squatted down to look.

'Sweet Marina, though I fall . . .' moaned the voice at her shoulder, but the sound was now so distorted that she could only make out the words because she already knew what they were.

It was soon after this that they began to come across the bones.

'We'll have to stop, Giles,' said Sarah. '*We* know about it, and what's what, but the police will have to be told, and come and take photographs, and arrange an inquest and things. Isn't it all dank and filthy and horrible? I'll be glad to get out, now.'

'Hang on a minute,' said Giles, resting on his spade. 'Let's reason it out. He was attacked here, in what must then have been a stable. That's feasible: Marina's brothers lurk out here in the dark, and wait until he comes to get his horse, and then jump out on him. Okay. They might easily decide to bury him then and there, because – yes, of course – a stable floor would be covered with straw and stuff, and the dug-up bit wouldn't be obvious once they'd put the straw back and horses had trodden over it. Now, he

was taking the brooch abroad with him, as a last
resort if he ran out of money. They'd have searched
his baggage, wouldn't they? And then thrown it
away somewhere. Probably down here, underneath.
But the point is, they didn't find the brooch, so it
wasn't in his baggage, and presumably it wasn't
anywhere in his clothes, either, because they'd have
had a pretty thorough look there, too, wouldn't they?
So what the hell had he done with it?'

Giles ran a grimy, sticky hand through his great
mane of coppery hair.

Polly began to feel slightly sick again, but the job
had to be done. Picking up a trowel, she lay down
and wriggled forward over the grave until she could
get her whole arm down into it, up to the shoulder.
Using sometimes the trowel and sometimes her
fingers, she began feeling about with the greatest
care, taking her direction from three or four greenish,
stick-like objects which she took to be ribs. Ribs
joining . . . a longish, knobbly piece . . . lost it . . . some
little loose bits, might be teeth . . . a larger, rounded,
smoother piece with holes in . . . and . . . Ah!'

Sarah began, 'What are you doing? I thought we
agreed to leave . . .' but stopped as Polly stood up and
slowly opened her clenched fist. Lumps of earth,
fragments of some sort of matted fibre – a glint of
gold.

Almost unbelieving, Giles and Sarah followed as
Polly went out to the tap in the yard and with infinite
care washed the brooch. The little gold mermaid and
merman sparkled in the sun for the first time in three
hundred years. All Polly said was:

'It's not quite clean, even now, and one of the pearl
drops has come loose, look, but I'm sure it can be put
right. Here you are, Giles.'

'But how did you *know*?' asked Sarah. 'That voice, was it?'

Polly smiled.

'No, much more ordinary. Giles's hair. I mean, if this wasn't in Who's-it's luggage or clothes, it must have been actually on himself. And then I looked at Giles and saw him push his hair back, and I thought, of course, they wore their hair long in those days, too, didn't they? And they didn't wash so much, I mean, it's not a nice thought but it would probably have been all sticky, so I thought, it would be quite possible for anyone with good thick hair to push something this size up into it, perhaps clip it in. It was an inspired guess, really.'

'It's an idea!' Giles grinned. 'I might use mine for smuggling watches or something.' He added, 'I said we were a prosaic lot, didn't I? All this hasn't put me off my lunch – I'm starving. How about you?'

First they phoned the Langwell police, who promised to be round within half an hour. After lunch, Giles remarked:

'I bet the local Press will be along, too. What are we going to say? Nobody's going to believe us if we tell them about Polly seeing and hearing things.'

Sarah agreed, and added:

'Another thing, Polly: if any of that got about, the papers would make a huge thing about it and you'd be plagued by all manner of crazy people wanting you to talk to dead relatives and find their family fortunes and a load of rubbish like that.'

'I know what,' said Polly. 'We can just say I met Giles by accident after visiting Hornabrook House, which is true, and we were talking about family history and the brooch was mentioned – also true – and we decided to look for it. They'll take it for granted that Giles already knew about the connection with Sapden Hall.'

'And,' added Giles, 'tell them about the bleeper, and they'll think we got the right spot by a combination of brilliant deduction plus electronics.'

He took out the brooch for another look.

'Must be worth a few thou,' he said. 'Wait till Sotheby's get this!'

'Oh, no – oh, Giles, you can't just sell it!' cried the two girls, and Polly wondered if Sarah had held similar ideas to her own about its possible future. Giles was exasperated.

'For pity's sake, what d'you expect? Put it in a glass case for visitors to gawp at, and pay out God knows what for insurance? Do you two realise that the money from this is my parents' only chance of getting a reasonably civilised standard of comfort? Look. If your people want to decorate a room, what do they do? Pop down to the nearest do-it-yourself shop, buy a few rolls of paper and pots of paint, spend the weekend on the job and it's done – right? Can you seen anyone doing that in a national monument? Oh, no. Submit plans, colour-schemes, get it costed, get hold of an approved contractor, wait while they put up scaffolding at umpteen pounds a day because the ceilings are so high, wait for a specialist to come and see if the plaster mouldings are okay, another one to see if there's bugs in the panelling, and when the bills come in – bang goes the cash you were hoping to get a decent carpet with, or some efficient radiators. I don't doubt there'll be a bit of legal hoo-ha over this brooch, but we're bound to benefit in the end.'

'I reckon from Marina's point of view, it's back where it belongs,' said Polly.

'Here's the police,' said Sarah. 'And – yes, *and* the press.'

After that they were kept very busy.

Some weeks later, Giles phoned Polly again.

'Just thought you'd like to know: it's okay about the brooch, and it's coming up at Sotheby's in a fortnight.'

'I'm sure Marina would be glad. It's pretty clear that she shared the family's practical outlook. I mean, all that about property, and inheriting things, and being willing to give the brooch away in a good cause.'

'I'm glad that's what you think. And Polly, you did say, didn't you, when the police had finally filled the grave in, that the voice had gone?'

'Quite gone. I say, Giles, do something for me?'

'Sure. Oh, and by the way, you should be getting something from my parents, too. There's going to be a little do at home, when we see how much the brooch fetches.'

'Oh, how lovely – I look forward to that. But what I was going to ask was: please will you try taking Ben up to the Long Gallery? If I'm right, he won't mind a bit. I just want to check that Marina's gone back out of time for good.'

The Little Yellow Dog

Mary Williams

In my mind I called him my sandman, because I always saw him at bedtime, from any window, when my Aunt Daphne had left me and gone downstairs. He was a small greyish yellow man, like the beach itself in the twilight, when the sea and sky became one . . . merging towards the dim uncertain lines of dunes tufted with beards of rush.

My aunt's seaside house stood high on the dunes, with only a small cluster of chalets and cottages straggling behind it to the village of Wyck-on-Sea. So I had a clear view from my window, and I always knew exactly when the old man would appear . . . immediately after the church clock had struck eight. The tower of the church poked up from the left on the sea-side of the hamlet, and I knew, with the queer instinct of children that he came from there.

I was just seven years old, and the old man was my secret, like the little yellow dog. The dog, though, was my daytime companion. We played hide and seek in the sandhills, and I only mentioned him once when my aunt came to find me for tea and said, 'Who were you calling to, Johnny?'

'The little yellow dog,' I said, 'look there he goes.' He was racing ahead, his rear end, with its fuzzy funny tail quickly disappearing round a hump of the dunes. But my aunt who was peering closely, said, 'There's *no* little yellow dog. You're making things up again. You mustn't. It's really silly.'

She wasn't pretending. She just didn't see him. That's why I didn't tell her about the sandman, because I knew it would be the same with him.

The shore at Wyck was wide and lonely, stretching for half a mile to the sea, when the tide was low, leaving just a few pools behind by occasional rocks and humps of mud.

Except for the dunes, everywhere round Wyck-on-Sea was flat. The roads and gardens seemed filmed always by thin sand, where poppies and star-shaped yellow daisy flowers grew profusely, in wild abandon. Dykes cut through the countryside, making a patchwork of fields rich with ripening corn and oats. There were butterflies too; hundreds of tiny blue butterflies flying and drifting on the hot air which was tangy with the smell of brine, seaweed, sweetbriar, and the bitter strange smell of the yellow daisy.

It was all so long ago; yet the atmosphere of that particular stretch of the east coast is as vivid to me now as it was then; and I can still see in my mind clearly, that dancing, laughing, raggedy-looking pup, and the more mysterious figure of the sandy-looking old man as he passed each evening along the beach, with his head turned up from his rounded back, his thin longish hair and beard blowing in the wind like the rushes of the dunes. Although I could not see his expression I knew he was looking for something. Once when I could not sleep I got out of bed later and went to the window. He was returning then from where he had been; his figure greenish gold in the moonlight, only more bent, as though he was saddened by great disappointment.

He walked . . . almost drifted along, with head bowed towards the glimmering sand, and when he reached the bend where the path led to the church, the shadows closed in on him and he was there no more.

The next day was sunny again; and when I told my aunt I was going to the beach, she looked at me doubtfully for a moment, then remarked, 'All right Johnny. Yes, it's a lovely day. Later perhaps I'll join you; so don't hide and pretend you're playing silly games with your make-believe little yellow dog.'

I didn't promise; I just nodded and was presently running through a valley of dunes with the blue butterflies all round me, the yellow daisies smelling, and the sand warm on my bare toes.

The tide was halfway out, and I wandered about for a bit, picking up razor-shells and some of the tiny pink ones that had holes in them, which I was collecting to give my sister Mary when I went home. She was recovering from chicken-pox, and would like them, I knew, if I could find enough for her to make a necklace.

I hadn't been out long when the little dog came racing towards me over a breakwater from the direction where the old man walked each evening. There was a funny little building there . . . a ruin . . . just under the sandhills, that someone said had been used in the war. The little dog was whitey-gold from sand, and when he jumped up at me, laughing, I could see the sand on his tongue, in his eyes, and on the shaggy brows falling over them. He never barked; and this, I thought, was why my aunt didn't believe in him. But then, ours was a secret relationship, and barking would have given the show away.

'Come on . . .' I called, starting to run with him beside me. . . . 'You hide and I'll find you. . . .' Generally he bounded off when I said that, but this time he didn't; just turned back in the direction he'd come from, paused, looked at me, then went on again. It happened several times until at last I followed, a bit grudgingly, because the dunes thinned that way, and weren't nearly so good for hide-and-seek, merging eventually into a part called The Warren, half sand, half earth and grass, and riddled with rabbit holes.

There weren't so many blue butterflies there, and quite suddenly as we approached the ruin, the sun went in, leaving the air cool with a thin wind shivering from the sea. The little dog hurried ahead, but I knew he wasn't playing hide-and-seek any more, although once, for a few seconds his shaggy form became lost in the grey light, and I felt suddenly sad with the queer kind of loss only a child could feel . . . as though all the magic had gone for good . . . all the magic I'd known of those summer haunted hours with the little yellow dog.

Then I saw him again; a shadowed shape slipping into the darkness of the derelict tumbled doorway.

I went in after him. He looked round once then started digging with his two front paws; digging with a hungry urgency that I knew in some way must be terribly important.

'All right,' I said, thinking of buried treasure. 'I'll help.' And my brief depression seemed to lift a little.

How long we scraped in the sand and earth I don't know. There'd been an exceptionally high tide that night, which had sucked a good deal of ground away, leaving rubble exposed that could have been hidden for years. Great chunks of coastline were being taken by the sea from time to time: my aunt had told me of a church and two empty cottages further on that had fallen and disappeared; that's why she didn't like me playing on the beach when the water was up.

I remembered this in my feverish attempts to help the little dog. He didn't seem to notice me any more, and he wasn't laughing, or playing, not even for a moment . . . just scrape, scrape . . . sniffing and scratching, until very gradually I began to get not only tired, but afraid, sensing intuitively the end of the adventure could be something less pleasant than pirates' gold.

So I got up, shook my clothes, and wiped the sandy dust from my eyes, knees and hands.

'I'm going,' I said. 'There's nothing there, anyway. It's a stupid game. I'm going home.'

I turned my head to look at him, but he wasn't there. He'd gone. I was sorry, and sad, and wanted to cry. He must have heard me when I was tidying and cleaning myself, and taken off without my noticing. I called and called, but there was no response. There was nothing left but the lonely shore outside the ruin, the far-off sea which had turned from blue to grey, and the lonely trek back across the sands, which seemed bereft without the little yellow dog.

That afternoon early, I took my bucket and spade and when my aunt questioned me, told her I was going to dig on the beach. 'Don't be long then,' she said, 'the tide's turned. If you're not back by three I shall come and fetch you.'

I went out, and as I cut through the dunes the blue butterflies were there again, and the sun was warm, diamonded gold and silver under the brilliant sky. But there was no little yellow dog, and he didn't even come when I reached the ruined hut or whatever it was, and started to dig with my spade.

I was hot, and soon my shirt was sticking to my back with perspiration. I could feel rivulets of sweat trickling from my forehead over my eyes and down my face. But the place where I found it, at last, was cold and damp from rain and sea, and the thing was shining white beneath the clinging rubble of dust.

I fetched some water in my bucket from a nearby pool, and threw it over the curled up shape. Then I stood staring. I wasn't frightened . . . just awed . . . the skeleton in a queer kind of way was beautiful in its perfection of bone structure, lying there as if in a long sleep . . . the skeleton which could so easily have been that of a little yellow dog.

I moved it very gently a few inches to the door of the ruined building, went out, and then looked back. In the sunlight the bones glistened clear and pale, like ivory. Perhaps I cried a little then, I don't know. But after the brief pause I walked on towards my aunt's house, not turning, not wanting to see any more . . . grateful only for the sunshine and distant sound of the waves breaking, for being alive in a world of summertime filled with blue butterflies and starred clumps of yellow daisy flowers.

That night I watched from my window as usual, and saw the sandy old man walking along the shore. He was hurrying this time, with his head turned to the twilit sky . . . or perhaps it was the wind at his back that made me think so . . . the wind and the thin clouds of fine sand blown upwards towards the

dunes. I went back to bed; but I was restless and
wakeful; and in about an hour ... it *must* have been an
hour ... because I heard the church clock chiming
nine ... I got up and crossed to the window again.

The moon was just spreading its path of silver
across the sea, gathering in radiance until the whole
scene was a brilliant pattern of light and slipping
shadows. It was then that I saw the old man returning, with something under one arm. Something that
looked like a sack. And as he passed, the colour of the
evening seemed to lift and change, momentarily
bathing the bent figure in a quivering glow of rose.
Everything suddenly was mysteriously warm and
comforting; and I knew then; knew something that
was beyond understanding, or the need to understand; sensed also, that in a few years I would be
beyond such knowledge, and must retain for as long
as possible its strange mystical awareness.

A minute later the enhanced translucence of the
sky faded once more into the pallor of moon-washed
dusk. The figure of the old man with his burden
slipped into the looming shadow of the church and
everything was still and motionless, and curiously
bereft.

Presently I went back to bed. I was tired, and slept
well. When I awoke, the morning sun was already
streaking through the curtains.

I got up, dressed and went downstairs, very quietly
so that my aunt, who was in the kitchen, would not
hear me. Then I let myself out of the front door, and
made my way by the dunes, to the church. The gate
was half open; I went through and up the path where
the gravestones stood on either side, emerging grey
and chillingly remote from the grass, only tipped yet,
with a glimmer of morning light; but the little yellow

daisy flowers were there, and a few poppies shedding their scarlet petals on the faint drift of wind.

It did not take me long to find the old man's resting place. I recognised it from the curled up carefully arranged skeleton of the little yellow dog which lay innocently close to a mound of grass topped by a simple stone.

With a lump in my throat I went closer and read the epitaph.

> Sacred to the memory of William Thomas
> born 1869 died 1939.

And lower down, smaller, and more frailly inscribed:

> In life he dearly loved his dog,
> and died mourning him.

Just then two tiny butterflies flew down from the sky. I held out my hand, and one fluttered and rested there for a second, velvet-bright in the morning dew.

Then I turned and went back to the house.

Later when I'd had breakfast, I returned to the churchyard. The pearly white skeleton no longer lay by the grassy mound. But a gardener was tidying up, and I wondered if he'd moved it away. It didn't matter because I felt everything was all right.

And that night I knew.

I saw them from my window, walking along the sands, just below the dunes. But the old man seemed taller, more erect, and gold in the golden light of evening, as gold as the little yellow dog trotting happily by his side. Once my sandman stopped and threw a stick, and I watched the little dog bound on after it, laughing, I was sure, as he'd laughed with me. I stayed at the window staring after them until the fading sky enfolded them, leaving nothing behind but the wide expanse of beach below the sandhills where the rushes blew.

I never saw them again; and no one else ever knew what had happened. In any case, no one really cared except me; the secret was mine alone . . . mine, the sandman's and of the little yellow dog who had been lost in the dunes, rabbiting, probably.

Sometimes, even now, after so many years, I look back and remember, reclaimed by that other world of blue butterflies and yellow daisy flowers . . . the world of childhood, where dreams so often have a potency for transcending physical reality, and perhaps more of truth.

Who knows?

I, for one, am not prepared to answer.

Glory Hole

Nicholas Fisk

'I wish it wouldn't keep making that noise,' Jo said. 'I hate it.'

The wall went *whooo, whoooo.*

'It's only the wind,' said her brother Bogey. A skateboarding scar on his lip gave him a Humphrey Bogart look: thus the nickname. His real name was Alec. He was almost sixteen, two years older than Jo.

The wall went *whooo, ooo, whoooo. . . .*

She grumbled, 'I know it's the wind, I didn't say it wasn't the wind. All I said was, I wish it wouldn't do it. It gets on my nerves.'

'Oh yes, your famous nerves . . .' Bogey said. Jo lowered her head so that her mane of brown hair fell forward, hiding her face. This meant she was upset. Bogey said more kindly, 'Look, it's only the east wind blowing through that gas-fire ventilator — the one Dad closed up. A sort of organ-pipe effect.' The wind went *whoooo. . . .*

Jo said nothing. She just twisted her hands about. Bogey began to feel peevish again. 'Look,' he said. 'If you're getting all sensitive and nervy, why don't you simply pick up your homework and simply do it in your own room? Or is that all too simple? If the wind gives you the wind up, why don't you blow?' His last words put him in a good temper again.

She threw her hair back and actually giggled. 'I'm sorry, I'm stupid, I know I'm stupid,' she said. 'But I really do hate that noise. Not just the noise – the *feeling* behind it. It's almost as if something or someone is *saying* things in the wall. . . .'

The wind went *whooo, ooo, ooo*.

'Saying what?'

'I don't know,' she said shuddering. 'Someone. Something. I'm talking nonsense.' She looked miserable again.

'All there is is a hole,' he said patiently. He listened to the noise. A voice? A something, a someone? Of course not. The wall went *whooo, whoooo*, and Bogey began to imitate it. 'Spooooooks . . . spoooky!' he crooned, grinning.

'Oh, shut up. Shut UP!' Jo said. The mane came over her face again.

'The voice of Doooo . . . ooom!' Bogey chanted.

'Shut up!' Jo shouted. She picked up her big dictionary and flung it with all her strength. Not at Bogey: at the patch of plasterboard on the wall. The book went *slam*. Bogey said 'What the —?' The wall said, '*Whooo, ooo, whooo* . . .'

Bogey, lips pursed, went to the plasterboard and inspected it. 'Now you've done it,' he said. 'You've bust the plasterboard. Dad *will* be pleased.'

'I haven't bust it,' she said. Her face was white. She looked at the damage. 'It's not broken at all,' she said 'It's just that filler stuff all round the edge. That's broken away.'

'And that's the bit Dad did so carefully,' Bogey said. 'Smoothing in the filler to make the edges nice and neat. Honestly, Jo. . . .'

She touched the broken fillet of filler. A whole piece fell away. She looked at Bogey, eyes wide with anxiety. The wall said, '*Whooo . . . ooo . . .*'

'Don't make such a fuss,' he said. 'Don't bother about it. I can fix it, you just take some filler and a knife and smooth it on.'

'It's the *paint*,' she said, tragically. 'You've got to match the *paint* . . .'

He began to laugh; she began to cry. 'You do like a good old tragedy, don't you, Jo?' he said, but kindly. She just sobbed. 'I'll mend it,' he said. 'I'll do it now. Look, cheer up, all I've got to do is pick off the old filler, put on the new and find the paint—'

'It's the noise,' she said. 'It's not the stupid plasterboard; Dad wouldn't make a fuss about that. It's the noise! I'm – I'm afraid of it!'

The wall went *Whooo, oooo. . . . whoo.*

'For heaven's *sake!*' he said, losing patience with her.

'But there's something there! Something inside! Don't touch it, don't do that!' He had taken hold of the board and was pulling it away.

'Just get out of the way,' he mumbled: and pulled hard.

The square of plasterboard came away with a dry crackle. Filler flaked and powdered and flew.

And there it was: the hole in the wall.

It looked at them and said, '*Whoooo, ooooo, whoooo . . .*' It sounded pleased.

It was all wrong.

It was a hole, yes. Sometimes you could see its

edges, its boundaries: you could see bricks, plaster, broken edges of lath. At these times it was just an ordinary hole.

But at other times, the hole seemed to shift – to move, to swell and contract, almost to breathe. Its edges, at these times, were not clear. As you looked, they wavered, fluttered, pulsed.

'Like a jellyfish . . .' Bogey said, at last. Jo said nothing. Like a cat, she extended her neck to look: then drew it back, offended and afraid. Her face was as white as the broken line of filler framing the hole. It went *Whooo, oooo!*, softly and invitingly.

Bogey put his hand towards the hole. 'Don't!' Jo said, sharply, seizing his wrist.

'Why not?' He looked at her almost sheepishly. He was afraid and did not want to show his fear. 'It's only a hole,' he said.

'It's not. It's—'

'It's what?'

'I don't know. Don't touch it. Don't put your hand in it.'

They stood staring at it. It wavered, shifted, pulsed, crooned. It opened and closed very slightly. Now it was blurred: the next moment, sharply outlined. It said, '*Whoooo* . . .' very gently.

At last Jo said, 'What are we going to *do*, Bogey?'

'What do you mean, do?' he said.

'Do with the hole. What do we do: just cover it up again? But we couldn't. I couldn't live with that *thing* there. Knowing it's there . . . there all the time. . . .'

'It's always been there all the time,' he said. 'You've managed to live with it till now, so you can go on living with it in future: when I've covered it up again.'

'No,' she said. 'No, don't cover it up.' Her eyes were wide.

'Why not?'

'I don't know. It's – it's not ready to be covered up yet.'

They had both been speaking in hushed voices. Now, Bogey spoke in his normal voice. 'Not ready?' he said. 'What a daft thing to say! How can it be ready or not ready? It's just a – a hole.'

'Not it's not,' she said. 'You know it's not.'

'What is it, then?'

She said, 'I don't know. No more do you. But don't cover it up.'

The hole softly said, '*Whoooo*. . . .'

Twenty minutes later, when they had finished inspecting the hole, making theories about the hole, watching it, trying to understand it, listening to its sounds and voices, Bogey said, 'Look, Jo, enough is enough. I know what you're thinking.'

She said, 'What am I thinking, then?'

'You want to *try* it. Find out if it *does* anything.'

She wouldn't look at him from behind her hair. She said, 'I'm not sure we should. But . . .'

'But you want to, don't you?' he insisted.

'I don't know. I don't like it. I don't trust it. Yes, I suppose I was thinking that.'

The hole wobbled, distorted, fluctuated. However hard you looked at it you could never see it clearly enough. Just when you thought you could see its true shape and size, it seemed to change again.

'What shall we give it, then?' he said. He took hold of her shoulder and pulled at her, making her look at him. Her eyes were as shifty and uncertain as the hole itself.

'Something that doesn't matter,' she replied. 'Something not . . . dangerous.'

He looked round the room. It was a small room; once it had been their nursery. Now it was the place where Bogey slept and he and Jo played records, did homework, stacked books and magazines. She had a little bedroom of her own. Her room was tidy most of the time. This room was a comfortable mess.

She said, 'The pencil mug. How about that?' and nodded her head at the cracked, striped china mug which held ballpoints and crayons and paintbrushes with matted bristles. He went to the mug and tipped everything out of it. She put her hand to her mouth and said, 'No, don't. I've changed my mind. Don't do anything—'

'Too late!' Bogey said, and threw the china mug into the hole.

The hole said, '*Whooo, ooo . . . whoo.*'

They looked in the hole. The mug had disappeared. Jo put her hand in, without thinking — realised what she was doing — drew back her hand and gave a little scream of fright. But her hand was undamaged, unchanged. She began to laugh, shakily.

Bogey laughed too. 'Well,' he said, 'it doesn't seem to mean us any harm . . .'

'But the mug has gone. Just disappeared.'

'It can't have done. Let's have another look.'

They looked again: looked carefully. The hole seemed to have no depth, or endless depth. It grew dark inside very quickly as if it soaked up light. Bogey found his torch and shone it into the hole. The hole seemed to swallow the light, to eat it, to soak it up.

Bogey said, 'Curiouser and curiouser.' Jo shivered and wrapped her arms round herself. But then, with a sort of sobbing sigh, she made herself look, with Bogey, along the beam of the torch, seeing as much of the hole as there was to see.

'There's something glinting,' she said.

'I can't see it. Where?'

'Something glinting! There!'

'You're imagining it. There's nothing there – wait a minute, though. . . .'

Something glinted in the hole. Or did it? Yes, it did. Just there, in the corner – no, there, in the middle—

The something became definite: cylindrical, round, glassy. A beautiful green tumbler.

They took it out and put it on the table where the light was bright and clear and looked at it, hardly daring to touch it.

'Do you think it really is glass?' Jo said.

'If it is, it's very good glass,' Bogey said. He held it in his hands now, and turned it between his fingers under the light. 'It's got a sort of petrol film of colours all over it . . . and it seems to change colour all the time, look. . . .'

'No, it's not changing colour, it's reflecting something. Give it to me.' She took the glass from him and inspected it. Its base was very thick and heavy: the glass – if it was glass – was thickest at the base, and almost opaque.

Jo said, 'Look! I'm right! You can just see it, buried in the base – something moving. That's why it seems to change colour.'

He snatched the glass from her, clumsily –

dropped it — saw it fall on the floor, bounce, roll. When he picked it up again, the beautiful glass was broken. A long curving crack curled round most of its side. He swore. Jo said, 'Well, it's no good going on like that, you've done it now. . . . Give it to me. I want to look at the base. At least you didn't break that.'

Shamefaced, he gave her the glass. She peered into it. He heard the sharp hiss of her breath when she gasped. 'Look!' she said. 'Look hard!'

He looked. Set in the base of the glass was a tiny crystal button. In the button was a golden worm. The worm spiralled and turned.

'It's like the filament of a torch bulb when the battery's almost flat,' he whispered. 'But it keeps turning and turning. . . .'

As he watched, the turning of the golden worm slowed — and Jo shook his elbow and said, 'Look, Bogey, look!'

'Where?'

'Look at the crack!'

He looked: and even as he watched, the crack mended itself. The hairline seemed to heal itself. The green glass was perfect again. The golden worm was only just turning.

Jo and Bogey looked at each other, wondering. At last she said, 'Let's put something in it and see if anything happens.'

'Put what?'

'Water. Milk. Anything. What have we got? There's this cold cocoa. . . .'

'Put that in.'

They put it in. Nothing happened. They waited and still nothing happened. Then Bogey said, 'I've an idea. Let's put the glass back in the hole with the cocoa in. I mean, the hole changed our china mug into a glass one, so it might change cocoa into another sort of drink.'

'I don't see why it should. I mean, there's no reason to suppose—'

'Don't let's argue. Let's just do it.'

They put the green glass in the hole. It disappeared. Two minutes later it reappeared. 'Nothing's happened!' Jo said, taking it out of the hole. Then she said, 'No: wait—'

Now, the glass was almost filled with a clear gold liquid.

Jo held the glass in her hands and smelled the liquid. 'Like fruit,' she said, holding out the glass for Bogey to smell. He said, 'Pineapple?' and stared at the liquid. It was very clear. So clear that you could see the golden worm in the button in the base turning, turning faster, turning so fast that it was spinning.

Jo said, 'It's cold! It's getting colder all the time!'

'What do you mean?' He took the glass from her. It was cold in his hand, so cold that the green glass frosted a little. Then the worm began to slow. It no longer spun, just revolved lazily.

Jo said, 'Go on, then. Try it.'

'You try it! I'm not going to poison myself! Ladies first!'

'You're scared!'

'I suppose you're not?' He handed her the glass. She made herself put it to her lips: then sip the golden drink. 'There!' she said. 'Your turn!'

He tried the drink. It was clean, clear and cold on his tongue. 'Like fruit,' he said. 'Fruit juices, mixed ... pineapple, or peach, or paw-paw, or everything mixed up. I don't know. It's a bit sweet.'

'Too sweet,' she said. 'That's why it's iced, I suppose. If it wasn't, it would be sickly. Do you feel funny at all?'

'No. Do you?'

'No. Let's finish it.'

They finished the golden drink, carefully watching themselves and each other for possible ill effects. There were none. 'I didn't think there would be,' Jo said. 'It wasn't that sort of drink, if you know what I mean. Poisons always taste, don't they?'

'I don't know. I don't really care,' Bogey replied. 'It's all too fantastic and amazing to worry about just being *poisoned*. . . .' He laughed. He dipped his finger into the glass to try and find a last drop of the golden liquid: he was still puzzled by its taste, which reminded him of every fruit and no fruit. He dipped his finger again and once again, then looked, puzzled, at his fingertip. It was dry.

'Not a trace of it left, Jo!'

She said, 'But the worm is turning again, fast. And the glass isn't cold any more. Do you suppose it's washed itself up?'

Bogey thought for a moment and said, 'Yes.'

'You don't sound very interested,' she said. 'I mean, a glass that chills drinks and washes up when you've finished drinking— '

'Oh, I'm interested all right,' Bogey said. He took the glass from her and stared at the golden worm.

'I'm interested all right,' he repeated. His voice was hard. 'Jo,' he said, after a pause, 'what have we got, to give the hole?'

She said, 'I don't understand you. What do you mean, "What have we got"?'

Bogey did not answer her. He jumped to his feet

and went from place to place in the room, picking things up and throwing them down. His face was set and determined. Jo said, 'What are you doing? Stop a minute and explain!'

He said, 'Peanuts . . . yes.'

'Look, what are you *doing*?'

'Ballpoint, we don't need that,' Bogey said. 'Ah! And a button – that's good!'

'Tell me what you're doing,' she demanded.

'You haven't got a needle and cotton?' he said, not listening to her.

'Yes, over there by the blue pot. But why—?'

He found the needle and cotton and added it to the other articles he had collected. They made a little pile in the palm of his left hand. 'Exploration kit,' he explained.

'I don't know what you're talking about! Stop looking so pleased with yourself and tell me what you're doing—'

He squatted beside her and tossed the handful of articles from hand to hand. 'It's obvious, isn't it?' he said, smiling quizzically at her. 'We've got a hole over there, right? And it seems to be a clever hole. I mean, we give it a rotten old china mug and it comes back with a beautiful glass tumbler that plays tricks, right? So it could be a hole full of goodies! A glory hole! And I intend to find out!'

She said, 'Wait a minute, Bogey, I don't like you in that mood—' but he did not listen. He went to the hole and threw in the salted peanuts. He crouched by the hole waiting to see what it would give him in return. Jo studied his face: good-looking, intelligent, even handsome except for the scarred lip. She looked at his mouth: he was biting his lower lip and so she could not see the impatient, almost greedy curl of his lips – the feature that betrayed his only real fault (and not such a bad fault as all that, she thought; he's not greedy or selfish where I'm concerned . . .).

'Ah!' he said – and reached into the hole, his fingers scrabbling for whatever it was that the hole gave him. . . .

His face fell. He opened his hand and showed her what the hole had returned. 'Peanuts . . .' she said. She would have laughed but the look on her brother's face stopped her. He stared at the peanuts and ate one. His face changed. 'Not salted!' he said. 'Not salted! Right! Fine! They know about peanuts, but they don't eat them salted!—'

'They?' she said. 'Who's *they*?'

But he was too busy to attend to her. 'Button,' he muttered, 'and needle and cotton. All right, hole. Try these!' He flung the button, needle and thread into the hole. His face was dark with excitement.

Jo said, 'What are you doing? Why those things?'

'Because buttons and a needle and cotton hold things together, stupid!' he said. 'And I want to find out how they hold things together – simple things, ordinary things. Surely you can see—'

'You keep on saying "They", who are *they*?'

'Look,' he said. 'The hole isn't just something on its own. It *belongs* to someone, it's a *useful thing* to someone.' He broke off to look into the hole. There was nothing in it yet. 'Don't you see,' he said to Jo, 'the hole is a sort of swap-shop. It's the means *they* use, whoever they are, to find out about *us*.'

'You can't prove that. It's just your opinion.'

'*They* want to find out about *us*, Jo. And *I* – I want to find out about *them*!'

There was a *whooo-ooo* from the hole, then the sound of something small, falling inside it.

The hole had given them two slips of material locked together.

The cloth was an unidentifiable synthetic, light as gossamer. One piece was blue, the other a pearly grey. When Bogey pulled them to tear them apart, they remained locked – yet there was no visible means of keeping them together: there was only, at the end of the pearly-grey piece, a tiny crystal button. Inside the button there twisted a golden worm.

'But this is all wrong!' Bogey complained. 'Buttons hold things together or let them apart. This stuff seems to be welded together and the worm-button is just an ornament.'

He pinched the button: the two pieces of material fell apart.

He placed the two pieces together again. The worm spun when he pinched the button. The two pieces joined as if sewn by an invisible thread.

Bogey whistled, and tried the trick again: then again. But it was Jo who saw how the trick was done. 'Look, Bogey. The worm changes direction. It reverses. Watch while I squeeze it to join the pieces.... Now watch again. The spiral's spinning downwards!'

'You're right!' he said; and was too excited to say more until, having made the pieces of material join and fall apart a dozen times, he said, 'So they know what they can do with their A's and O's!' and began to chuckle.

'What has all this got to do with A levels and O levels?' Jo asked him.

'Dad seems to think I won't get any, and old

Badger at school seems to think I won't get enough,' Bogey said, bitterly.

'Dad never said you wouldn't get any, he just wants you to work harder to get as many as possible.'

'Yes, I know what he "just wants". And I know what Badger wants too — bags of A's and O's to swank about, "Oh what a wonderful school I run!"' He began to chuckle again while making the crystal button do its trick.

'Well, anyhow,' Jo said, 'what's all that to do with the hole in the wall?'

'If I were as rich as Croesus, everyone would love and respect me. Especially me,' he said, raising an eyebrow at Jo. 'They wouldn't ask me about A's and O's,' he continued. 'They'd just bow from the waist whenever I swept past in my Lamborghini and hope I'd drop a few fivers for them to pick up.' He began to sing. '*Money, money, money. . . .*'

'And where's all this money coming from?' Jo said, trying to disapprove of her brother, but finding it difficult. She liked his wild schemes. The wilder the better. They never harmed anyone. They made life exciting.

'From the hole in the wall,' he said, suddenly serious. 'Glory hole.'

'You're joking!'

'I'm not. Look, I'm fifteen. That's too young to get what I want, but old enough to be a disappointment.'

'You're not a disappointment; that's stupid! Dad and Mum expect you to try for a reasonable number of A's and O's; everyone's parents expect that! They're not expecting you to be *rich*!'

'I wasn't expecting me to be rich until this evening. I wasn't expecting to get many A's or O's either. And I'm still not.'

'Well, you won't get rich simply because of the hole in the wall. I mean, it's ridiculous! And *you're* being ridiculous, sitting there all piggy-eyed and greedy-faced, talking about Lamborghinis. A clapped-out old Mini, that's what you'll have.'

He stood above her, furious.

'You've got as much imagination as a bath sponge!' he shouted. 'Can't you see? Can't you *see*? If only we can get hold of enough golden worms – and find out just how they work, what makes them do things – if I can do that, everything's mine! The whole world! It's like discovering the wheel, and radio, and the sewing machine. . . . It's like having a whole new world fall into your lap!'

She stared up at him, appalled. He really meant it. He was serious. The wall crooned, '*Whooo . . . oooo*' in the dying wind.

There was a scratching at the door. Glad not to have to look at her brother's face any longer, she went to the door and let Tiddles enter. She picked him up and buried her face in his comfortable furry neck.

When she looked at her brother again, his back was to her. He was offering the hole his transistor radio. He's going mad! Jo thought, remembering how he had saved up for the little radio. As if to prove her right, Bogey jerked his record player's flex out of the wall and took the machine to the hole. It won't go in, it's too big for the hole! she thought.

But somehow the hole wavered and fluttered and expanded: and the record player disappeared in its darkness.

Much later, she lay awake in her own little room. The wind was almost dead now. The night was still except for the occasional small noises from Bogey's room. She knew what he was doing. He was feeding still more things into his Glory Hole.

She was tired of it; bored with the miracle; frightened by Bogey's fixed, pale face, the avid glare of his eyes. When she had left him, the transistor radio had been returned as a little shining nugget of mixed metals, some bright, some dull. Three golden worms powered it. Bogey muttered at it, pushing the various facets of the metal casing – until suddenly the room filled with the sound of his own voice, a playback of the words he had spoken.

And the record-player. The hole offered nothing in exchange for it. Jo thought she knew why. The little nugget could contain a radio, record-player, tape-recorder and a dozen other things that *They* found amusing or useful. Bogey must have thought the same. 'Not good enough for you, is that it?' he'd muttered. Throwing the nugget behind him, he fed the Glory Hole his automatic camera: and the hole had returned a black box, almost flat and about half the size of a box of matches. Three golden worms turned at the corners. A fourth worm seemed to be the lens.

'But I don't see what it's supposed to do!' Bogey had stormed. 'I don't see how it works!' Seeing the despair in his face and the fury behind the despair, she thought: I've had enough. Too much. And left.

She turned uneasily in her bed, trying to get comfortable. Her pillow felt hot, the bedclothes felt heavy. She reached out a hand for Tiddles, who always lay in the same place on her coverlet. She needed the purring warmth of the cat to console her for the picture in her mind of her brother's face. He wants something for nothing, she thought; you never get that. But then she thought: But you do, don't you? You get the warmth of a cat for nothing, the feel of its fur, the sound of its contented purring. . . . Come on, Tiddles. Cheer me up.

He wasn't there.

The place where he lay was still warm. Where was he? Of course: the dim light of the hall shone through the chink of her slightly open bedroom door. He had deserted her – stretched his back, yawned, plopped silently from bed to floor, then padded his delicate way downstairs. By now he was most probably sitting, erect and unblinking, by the door in the kitchen that led to his food. His eyes would fix, accusingly, on anyone who came near him. His mouth would open to give a strangled, high-pitched mew that meant, 'I suffer. I starve. I demand action!'

Jo smiled and fell asleep with this picture in her mind.

It was the wrong picture.

Tiddles was with Bogey, watching the boy with clear, gold, emotionless eyes as he strode about the room trying to find new things, revealing things, to feed to the Glory Hole.

He gave it a pair of compasses . . . a magnifying glass . . . a spanner.

The Glory Hole replied with nuggets and boxes and jewellery-like objects, each with one or more golden worms, that made no sense.

And yet . . . and yet! For the compasses, the hole offered a little bronze box that displayed changing characters. Not Roman, Egyptian or Arabic – just symbols. When Bogey placed the box by a right angle, the characters promptly glittered with intelligence, giving him a message he could not understand. Placed between two books, the box seemed to measure the gap separating them. But did it? *Did* it?

For the spanner – nothing. The spanner was simply returned to the hole.

For the magnifying glass – another mystery: the hole gave him a smooth, crystal-like plate, completely transparent. A single golden worm was set in one corner. By squeezing this tablet or plate, he could see magnified images. The harder he squeezed, the greater the magnification. So the tablet was like a flexible glass lens. What use was that? No use at all that Bogey could see. He put the thing to one side and suddenly it glowed with light. On the ceiling there appeared a sharp, magnified image – then another – and then a whole string of them, one after the other. Amazing!

But the images were useless. They showed only what Bogey had put before the magnifier. 'Why won't you show me something of *yours*, something from *your* world?' Bogey muttered.

He thought: They could be laughing at me, these people – or things . . . They could be teasing me. Taking, but never giving. Showing, but never explaining. I give them photographs of myself – but no pictures of *Them* ever come back: just geometrical figures that move when I watch them and tell me nothing. Nothing!

Why won't they tell me what they are like? They must be animal in some way, mustn't they? Only animal beings – beings like humans – would need tools and instruments and glasses to drink from? And they have cloth, so they wear clothes made of materials that fasten and unfasten. . . .

But perhaps not. An armchair is 'clothed' in fabric, but an armchair isn't an animal being. . . .

He picked up a photograph of himself that he had already put in the Glory Hole, and wrote across it, with a black felt-nib pen:

ME!
HUMAN ANIMAL
YOU?
WHAT ARE YOU?

He put the picture in the Glory Hole and waited, biting his nails. After the usual delay when the picture disappeared, something formed in the hole: something flat. . . .

It became clear and sharp. He took it out. It was his picture, unchanged, unaltered, and accompanied with – nothing.

He stared dully in front of him with the picture in his hand. He had to know: they were not going to tell him.

He felt something touch his knee. Tiddles. He said, 'Oh, go away, leave me alone.' The cat rubbed harder at his knee and gave a chirruping miaow. He said, 'Shut up. You know where the food is, go and get it.' The cat mewed louder and straightened its tail, hooking the tip sideways to show it was offended. It walked away from Bogey, stiffly, and thrust its head towards the Glory Hole with a sort of disgusted curiosity: then prepared to leave.

'Wait a minute!' Bogey said. 'Wait a minute, Tiddles . . . You're a fine cat, aren't you?' He stroked the cat's chin. 'You're a splendid animal, aren't you?' The cat narrowed its eyes and purred.

'Come with me, Tiddles,' Bogey said.

He put the cat in the Glory Hole: sealed the hole with the piece of plasterboard: and prepared to wait.

Surely he would get an answer now?

After two minutes, the answer came. Trembling, Bogey removed the plasterboard – and Tiddles, the same old Tiddles, jumped out of the hole and ran from the room, ears back.

'All right,' Bogey said. 'All right, all *right*! I'll see for myself!'

Jo awoke suddenly. It was Tiddles. He kept mewing. Not in his usual ways: he sounded as if he were trapped, or injured.

She turned on her bedside light. The cat was there all right – there by the cupboard. Its ears were flat on its head and its eyes very round. It scratched at the cupboard, then changed its mind and ran under her bed. She put her hand down and said: 'Tiddles! Come out! What's wrong?' The cat scratched her and spat.

She jumped out of bed, got down on hands and knees, lifted the blankets and sheets and saw Tiddles. He backed away from her, eyes blazing – then mewed and butted her hand with his face. But he would not let her pick him up; he kept trying to find another place to go. She had never seen him like this. 'Tiddles,' she said. 'Don't be silly, come on now, don't be silly . . .'

Then she remembered about the hole.

Bogey's room was completely silent. Heart beating, she opened the door. The cat ran between her legs – into the room – out again, spitting, its fur raised. She said, 'Bogey!' He was not there. Everything was silent but for the sounds Tiddles made. He was running, mewing, scrabbling, doing a dozen meaningless, panic-stricken things.

She was going to call her brother's name again when she saw his feet. Only his feet. They were sticking out of the hole.

She tried to scream but no sound came. She tried to move but could not. She was frozen, with one hand clutching her throat, the other stretched out, like claws, towards his feet, over there, across the room, coming out so slowly from the Glory Hole. . . .

They were not his feet! Not *his*, only like his. The feet, the ankles, the legs – the hole seemed to be giving birth to him, or the thing that was not him: the white, clean, perfect, horrible thing, the thing she wanted to scream at—

At last it was over, and he – it – lay there, complete, on the floor under the hole. Motionless, but for the fluttering of the petal-like eyelids. Glimmering white, smooth, flawless, hairless. Him. Not him. His head seemed larger. Too large. His scarred lip was still healing: as she watched, the last of the scar faded and vanished leaving only rose and white perfection.

He groaned and rolled from side to side: then completely over. She felt the burn of vomit in her throat when her eyes were trapped by the sight of the crystal buttons, in which turned little golden worms, in his neck, his brow, his belly, his chest. His eyelids fluttered again. They opened: then she saw the spiralling gold worms in his eyes.

*

Later, when the dawn showed grey through the curtains, she knelt by him. Her hands were calm in her lap. She had made her mind tranquil. But though she could listen to him when he spoke to her in his new, high, melodious voice, she still could not bring herself to look at him.

He began to talk again, saying in different words the same old thing. 'Jo! It worked! It's all mine now!'

'Yes, I know,' she said. 'You told me. I'm glad, Bogey.'

'It worked!' he said. 'I won! Didn't I, Jo?'

'Yes,' she said. 'Of course you did.'

'I fooled them, Jo. Got their secret. . . .' His voice was tired. It was some time before he spoke again. And this time, there was the first hint of doubt when he said, 'They're very strange, Jo. Not like us. Not like us at all.'

'I know,' she said.

'They're more like – more like *machines*. . . .' The perfect white body, too small for the head, twisted uneasily. The worms spiralled busily and soothed it, adjusting its warmth, its blood flow, its everything. When next he spoke his voice was stronger.

'They made me very welcome!' he said. 'They really were glad to see me! You'd be surprised how glad, Jo. . . .'

'No, I wouldn't,' she said. And added, quickly, 'Of course they were glad to see you, Bogey.'

'You see, they *needed* me, Jo. They *wanted* me. They said so. Often.'

He tried to get up but his new limbs and body would not work for him. She had to help him to his feet. Her lips were compressed and her eyes hard and bright.

'So it's all ours now, Jo!' he said.

'Very nearly, Bogey, very nearly,' she answered: and came to her decision. 'We're almost there, yes. But you've still got to get it for yourself. Remember, Bogey? It's in there. In the hole. It's all waiting for you, there!'

She guided his hands and arms, then his head, into the hole, encouraging him softly. It hurt her to touch him. His flesh was not flesh but something soft and smooth, perfect and hideous and alien. He struggled feebly but willingly to help her.

At last only his white, shapely feet remained. Shivering, she wrapped her hands in the hem of her nightdress – seized his feet – and pushed.

He was gone.

She ran to her room and searched frantically for her crucifix. She had not worn it or thought about it since her childhood and could not find it. Her work-box – it might be there. It was. She took it and hurried to the hole.

There she knelt, clutching the crucifix.

'Please, God,' she whispered. 'Please, God, please! Into Thy hands, oh Lord! Into *Thy* hands! Please!'

But she doubted He would listen.

Acknowledgements

The authors and publishers would like to thank the following people for giving permission to include this anthology material which is their copyright:

Margaret Biggs for 'The Ghost of Rainbow Hill'.
Fontana Paperbacks for 'Lost Goldmine' by Hazel F. Looker from *Welsh Ghost Stories*.
Hodder and Stoughton Australia for 'The Ghost of Gartenschmuck' by Colin Thiele from *A Handful of Ghosts*, and for 'Katzenfell' by Christobel Mattingley from *Spooks and Spirits*.
Jan Mark for 'Who's a Pretty Boy, Then?' from *Dark Eyes and Other Spine Chillers* published by Bell and Hyman, © Jan Mark 1981.
Penguin Books Ltd for 'The Strange Illness of Mr Arthur Cook' by Philippa Pearce from *The Shadow Cage and Other Stories* (Puffin 1978). Text copyright © Philippa Pearce 1977.
Victor Gollancz Ltd for 'Time to Laugh' from *A Touch of Chill* by Joan Aiken.
Judith Butler for 'Time, and Time Again' from *Young Winter's Tales 3* (Macmillan).
William Kimber and Co Ltd for 'The Little Yellow Dog' from *Chill Company* by Mary Williams (William Kimber 1976).
Nicholas Fisk for 'Glory Hole' © 1978 Nicholas Fisk. First published by Macmillan in *Young Winter's Tales 8*.

More Beaver Books

We hope you have enjoyed this Beaver Book. Here are some of the other titles.

Ghostly Laughter A Beaver original. The chief characters in this unusual collection of stories are ghosts with a difference – they are so eccentric and lovable they will make you laugh! Chosen by Barbara Ireson, the stories are a hilarious and thrilling read for the nine-and-over age group

The Beaver Book of Creepy Verse A Beaver original. A fascinating collection full of ghosts, ghouls, witches, monsters, ogres, spells and curses – some terrifying, some funny – and all guaranteed to send a shiver down your spine. Chosen by Ian and Zenka Woodward and chillingly illustrated by William Geldart

Creepy Creatures A Beaver original. Nine stories about *nasty things* to make your flesh creep and your hair stand on end! Collected by Barbara Ireson

Ghostly and Ghastly A Beaver original. Thirteen stories of ghostly happenings collected by Barbara Ireson and illustrated by William Geldart make a spine-chilling read for everyone from nine upwards

These and many other Beavers are available from your local bookshop or newsagent, or can be ordered direct from: Hamlyn Paperback Cash Sales, PO Box 11, Falmouth, Cornwall TR10 9EN. Send a cheque or postal order for the price of the book plus postage at the following rates:
UK: 45p for the first book, 20p for the second book, and 14p for each additional book ordered to a maximum charge of £1.63;
BFPO and Eire: 45p for the first book, 20p for the second book, plus 14p per copy for the next 7 books and thereafter 8p per book;
OVERSEAS: 75p for the first book and 21p for each extra book.

New Beavers are published every month and if you would like the *Beaver Bulletin*, a newsletter which tells you about new books and gives a complete list of titles and prices, send a large stamped addressed envelope to:

Beaver Bulletin
Arrow Books Limited
17–21 Conway Street
London W1P 6JD

9337703